YA-F SHA
Zom-B bride
Shar, Darren

D0340511

ZOM-B BRIDE

COMING SOON

ZOM-B BRIDE

DARREN SHAN

HarperCollins*Publishers*Ltd

Published by HarperCollins Publishers Ltd

First published in Great Britain in 2015
by Simon & Schuster UK Ltd
A CBS Company

First Canadian edition

HarperCollins Publishers Ltd
2 Bloor Street East, 20th Floor
Toronto, Ontario, Canada
M4W 1A8

www.harpercollins.ca

Library and Archives Canada Cataloguing in Publication
information is available upon request.

ISBN 978-1-44341-535-4

Printed and bound in the United States
RRD 9 8 7 6 5 4 3 2 1

THEN . . .

Life was hard for Becky Smith — but death was a lot harder. Attacked, killed and turned on the day zombies first ran riot across the globe, B recovered consciousness months later as a revitalised member of the undead, and soon found herself at the centre of a war to decide the future of the world.

On the side of good stood Dr Oystein and his team of Angels, determined to rid the world of its undead stain and return control to the living. On the side of chaos and villainy stood Mr Dowling and his band of merciless mutants. The killer clown spread disorder and death wherever he pranced.

Slotting in around the forces of good and evil were a variety of other groups and individuals. The Ku Klux Klan became a major player, backed by remnants of the army. Both were in league with the

Board, a cluster of powerful, ruthless tyrants who saw the world as their plaything. And an owl-eyed, semi-undead man seemed to have a finger in every slice of the action.

A pair of vials lay at the heart of the feuding factions. One contained a virus which could wipe out every zombie on the face of the earth within a couple of weeks if released. The other held a virus which would finish off the last living survivors just as swiftly. Dr Oystein had explained to B that he held the zombie-destroying virus, but that Mr Dowling was in possession of its counterpart.

Though the opposing sides could parry and jab at one another, they couldn't declare all-out war while the vials were in the hands of their respective owners. If the Angels targeted Mr Dowling and were poised to crush him, he could release his virus in retaliation. Similarly, if Mr Dowling or Owl Man launched an assault on the doctor's base in County Hall, Dr Oystein could uncork his vial and disperse the fumes that would wipe out the undead. It was a twisted stalemate, and at times it looked like there might be no way forward.

B had suffered greatly as a revitalised, but nobody hurt her as much as Dan-Dan, a child-killer who held her captive in Battersea Power Station and tore her body to shreds, extracting every last tremor of pain that he could.

Just when it looked as if B was finished, she was spared by the most surreal of saviours — Mr Dowling. The crazed clown had crossed paths with her twice before, and saved her from her enemies both times. Invading Battersea Power Station with an army of mutants, zombies and eerie babies, he rescued her yet again, and asked her to come with him, claiming that she belonged by his side, that he was going to take her *home*.

B was weary and in agony. She had been betrayed and tortured. Her parents had both perished in the battle at the Power Station. She was alone, fragile, bewildered. Mr Dowling promised to spare the human survivors in the building if she went with him. In that time of madness and grief, he was the only one to offer her a helping hand, and she seized it gladly. It didn't matter to her that he might be – as

Dr Oystein believed – an agent of pure, satanic evil. She was a fallen Angel and, in her distressed state, it seemed only natural for her to accept the aid of a demon.

So B struck a Faustian pact with Mr Dowling and let herself be lifted on to the shoulders of dozens of blank-eyed, sharp-fanged babies, the most unusual of the clown's mutant creations. Crooning to her softly, they carried B like a holy relic, out of the crumbling Power Station, down a tunnel into the darkness of their underground lair.

NOW . . .

ONE

You know what? I'm enjoying this! I feel like a princess being borne aloft by her personal retinue. A welcome treat after what I've endured recently. I'm in no hurry for it to end. Part of me wishes it could last forever. If this was what the afterlife was like, a calm procession through the unending gloom, I'd sign up for it in a heartbeat. If, of course, I had a heart.

The babies transfer me carefully, lovingly. They're silent most of the time, but occasionally they'll murmur, '*we love you mummy.*' It's almost like an incantation. It soothes and comforts me. I can't recall why I used to think it was menacing when they crooned it in my nightmares when I was alive.

There's no sign of Mr Dowling or his mutants. I hope they kept their promise and herded the zombies out of the Power Station, giving the surviving humans inside a chance to organise themselves, free the locked-up slaves and retreat. Maybe I should have asked to stay behind to oversee the exodus. With hindsight, I suspect I agreed too quickly to their offer. I've no way of telling if they upheld their end of the bargain.

Then again, why should I be expected to do everything? I'm so tired and in so much pain. I've done all that I can to help. I can't see every last stage of a rescue operation through to its end. Others have to step up and take responsibility too, don't they?

I wish I didn't care. It must be so easy to be a selfish creep like Mr Dowling, Dan-Dan or Rage. All I want is to enjoy the comfort of the dark and my strange journey through it. But my thoughts keep returning to the Power Station. I'm troubled. I don't trust the clown and his followers. They could do anything.

'*don't cry mummy,*' the babies whisper, sensing my unease. '*going home mummy. we love you. it will be all yummy now.*'

Yummy mummy, I think to myself, and the babies laugh softly.

'*yes. yummy mummy. we love you yummy mummy. forever ours.*'

How strange that they picked up on that. We must have a mental connection. They're reading my thoughts, at least to an extent. That should scare me, but it doesn't. In fact it makes me chuckle warmly. I want to pull the little guys in close and hug them. They seem so lovable and cute. I know they're not. I haven't forgotten about the artist, Timothy Jackson, or the people they slaughtered at Battersea Power Station. They're deadly killers, regardless of their tiny size. But they've yet to threaten me. Just because they used to tear me apart in my dreams doesn't mean they want to kill me in real life.

I hope!

I've no idea where we are or how long we've been trudging through the dark. I haven't tried to keep

11

track of time. We might have been down here for twenty minutes or a few hours.

Every now and then, a shaft of light finds its way down to us. I glimpse brick walls, open sewers, the occasional shredded corpse, bones scattered about the place, dried bloodstains, the babies trudging through the mess, taking no notice as the hems of their white christening gowns become soiled. I'm worried in case they pick up germs and get infected. Then I remember that they're not ordinary children. I think it would take more than a bit of filth to trouble these fierce, sexless warriors.

There are rats down here, scores of them, hiding in the dark depths where even the undead don't tread. I catch glimpses of them when light pierces the blackness, gnawing on bones, stripping them of their last few scraps of flesh. Some are the size of a small dog. I don't think a human or zombie would last long in this kingdom of rodents. The rats would tear any normal intruder to shreds.

But the feral creatures run scared of the babies. They flee, squealing, snapping wildly at one another, the stench of their terror thick in the air. They must have had run-ins with the babies in the past, and come off the worst.

The babies ignore the rats and march along merrily, only pausing when they have to negotiate an obstacle or transfer my motionless body to another level. They're incredibly gentle whenever they pass me into fresh hands, whispering to assure me that everything is fine. *'don't worry mummy. we won't drop you mummy. we'll keep you safe forever.'*

I don't know how they find their way in the dark, but they maintain a steady pace. They never stop at a junction to consider their options. It's always full speed ahead, taking turns in their stride as if following directions on a satnav. For all I know, they are. Maybe Mr Dowling inserted a homing beacon in each of their tiny heads. Perhaps it's just instinct. Or one of them might have a map.

I giggle at the thought of the babies crowding together over a map. They laugh softly in response and I feel a wave of warmth seep through me. I'm not sure if I'm imagining it or if they transmit heat when pleased.

My thoughts start turning towards my parents, Dad's face as he shut the door on me and steeled himself for the end, how he must have settled down beside my zombie mother as he pulled the pin on the grenade that he always carried, setting them both free of this hard, cruel world. With an effort, I block out those grisly memories. There will be plenty of time to mourn later. I'm too weary to deal with my loss right now.

Instead I make myself think about Dan-Dan. That's more pleasant. The world is well rid of the sicko. I love that he cowered at the end. He put on a brave front most of the way, but he couldn't keep up the pretence when his time came. He died terrified and pitiful, the way a monster of his kind should.

The eyes of the babies light up around me, a dim red glow in the gloom. '*dan-dan*,' they growl.

'It's OK,' I calm them. 'He's gone now.'

The light fades and they push on, but that's another sign that they're tuned into my thoughts. It's just as well that I'm at ease in their company and happy to be going along for the ride. I'm not sure how they'd react if I started plotting ways to strike at them.

But what if I plotted attacks on other people? If they'd been around when I was locking horns with Dan-Dan, I'm sure they would have taken my side and made short, bloody work of the giggling monster. I wonder if they'd back me against my other foes too?

To test my link with the babies, I focus on a memory of Mr Dowling tormenting a woman and her baby in Trafalgar Square. My fear and hatred of him resurface as I recall how he tricked her and turned her child into a zombie. As dark feelings rumble through me, I wait for the babies' eyes to turn red again.

They don't. Instead the babies titter, then trill, '*daddy.*'

Looks like I'll have to rely on myself when I cross swords with the mad clown later. Typical. Where's the SA bloody S when you need them?

TWO

After a long trek through London's charming waste system, we nudge into what feels like a much larger tunnel. Even though it's pitch-black, I can tell we're no longer in the sewers. The babies' feet don't splash in putrid puddles, and echoes are tinnier. Plus the smell has faded.

As we progress, I spot light far ahead. I raise my head, but it's too far off to make out any details, so I lie back and wait, humming tunelessly to myself.

The glow increases as we march towards the mouth of the tunnel. The roof and its array of pipes and cables swim into focus. I'm familiar with areas like this, so I know now where we are. It's a Tube line, one of the maze of underground tunnels which used to play host to trains packed with commuters in the old days.

'Choo-choo!' I croak.

The babies copy me. '*choo-choo mummy. choo-choo.*'

'Good babies,' I murmur. 'Let's try another one.' I start singing, 'The wheels on the bus go round and round,' but the babies don't take up the tune. Maybe they don't like that song. Or maybe they never saw a bus in action. If they were born after mankind fell, the song would mean nothing to them.

There's no telling how old the unnatural infants are. I'm assuming that, like zombies, they age slowly. If that's the case, they could be as old as I am, or older. Maybe they're adults, trapped in the bodies of babies, decades shy of reaching maturity.

We pass from the tunnel into the light and I have to fling an arm over my eyes to shield them from the glare. My vision starts to adjust as we move along, and after a while I'm able to lower the arm and take in my surroundings.

We're passing through a Tube station. I raise my head and spot a sign with the name Temple on it. I sometimes swept through here on a train from the East End. We're not that far from County Hall.

There are grunting sounds and I look around. Loads of zombies are standing at the edge of the platform, staring at us. Some of them have cocked their heads in confusion, and I can tell they don't know what to make of us.

The zombies disturb my tranquillity and set me thinking about my situation. I should probably consider making a break for freedom. The Tube station would be a good place to do it, since it provides an exit to the world above, as well as lots of bodies to knock over and stir up into an agitated mob, in the hope that they might provide a barrier between myself and the babies. But I'm a physical wreck and there are dozens, maybe hundreds of babies. Even if they couldn't read my thoughts and nip any escape plan in the bud, they'd catch me long before I made

it to the platform. I'd be wasting my time and what little energy I have left. Besides, as I've already noted, I'm enjoying this in a strange kind of way. I'll worry about escape another time.

As I turn away from thoughts of freedom, I notice that one of the undead spectators on the platform is wearing a train conductor's outfit. I laugh with delight and wave at him. 'Tickets, please!' I yell.

The conductor's lips move automatically as a memory kicks in and he tries to mimic the cry, but he can't make any sensible sounds. He holds out a hand and I feel sorry for the glum-looking jobsworth. I wish I had a ticket or an Oyster card that I could flash at him. That would make his day. Even better than a bowl of fresh brains.

I'm surprised the lights work down here. But that's the way it's been since humanity's downfall. Nothing works in some places, but in other areas televisions and radios crackle away, lights shine through the night and day and the world carries on as if there's still someone at the rudder, directing it all.

I expect the zombies to hop down to check me

out, but they must be able to tell from their vantage point that I'm undead, because not one of them approaches. Glancing down at my torso, I realise why. Though most of my ribs are bandaged over, the area around my chest is clear. They can see the hole where my heart should be, along with the fresh, gaping wound where Dan-Dan recently sliced off my right breast.

I wince at the memory of the assault. I was never a girly girl. I didn't worry about make-up, dresses, stuff like that. But with my ruined chest there's now nothing at all to mark me out as female, not unless I was to drop my drawers. I feel like I've become an androgynous, meaningless thing, like the sexually neutral babies.

'Sexless Smith,' I laugh weakly. 'That should be my new name.'

The babies stop before exiting the station. They hold perfectly still and I get the feeling they're communicating with one another. That's confirmed a second later when one of them – the one with a hole in its head, the baby I'm pretty sure Timothy rescued – steps away from the others and addresses me directly. *'are you hungry mummy? we can make the dead people bring you brains.'*

'That's sweet of you,' I smile, 'but I ate not long before you invaded the Power Station. I'll be fine.'

The baby nods, resumes its place in the pack and they proceed. I wave goodbye to the zombies as we leave. As Mum always said, it pays to be polite.

Back into darkness. It doesn't bother me. In fact I prefer it to the light. I can't see the wreckage of my body in the gloom, and the pain doesn't seem so bad. I don't want a ship and a star to sail her by. I want a coffin and an eternity of quiet black.

We come to a train on the tracks. Lights flicker on and off inside the carriages. I expect the babies to edge around, but they climb in and escort me through the train. It's littered with corpses. I guess the zombies in the station, or others like them, found these guys after they got marooned here on the day the world fell.

I try to imagine what it must have been like for the passengers, stuck down here, not sure what was happening above, waiting, hot, suffocating. Maybe some people chose to leave and walk along the tracks to the nearest station, but most stayed, confident that someone would come to sort things out, as they always did. Then the undead forced their way in. The killing commenced. Nowhere to hide. Nowhere to run.

'It was the same up top,' I whisper to the skeletons. 'Most of you would have died even if you'd got out. At least this way you have a ready-made tomb. The people up above simply lie rotting on the streets.'

There are more rats in the carriages, though they don't linger when they catch sight of the babies. They take off as if the place is on fire. A few of the babies dart after them and bite the heads off any that they catch, but most hold their position beneath me.

The rats set me thinking. I bet they're not the only animals at large. The tunnels have long been home to rodents, but I'm sure they've been joined by others since zombies took over. Dogs, cats, foxes ... The smarter animals would have headed for far-flung, deep-buried holes like this, where they could rest unseen from their brain-hungry predators.

Many of the furry survivors who sought shelter here probably still emerge in the daytime to hunt for food. But there are surely others who will have made the darkness their full-time home. Maybe they'll breed blind puppies, kittens and cubs, better equipped for hunting underground. This could be the start of a new evolutionary chapter, the era of the sightless.

I pass the time thinking about that, picturing myself as a modern Darwin, charting the changing face of the animal kingdom. It keeps me amused as we follow the tunnel through Cannon Street Station, Monument, Tower Hill.

I recall the undead Beefeater who wrestled me to the ground and demanded a ticket before letting me enter the Tower of London. Is he still at his post? Surely not, after all this time. Then again, he seemed like a determined sort. It wouldn't surprise me if he'd stuck to his guns. I try asking the babies to swing by that way, so I can check, but they press on without pause, ignoring my pleas to make a short detour.

The line branches after Tower Hill. One set of tracks curves off to the north, but we follow those that lead east, towards what used to be my home turf. I wonder if that's where the babies plan to take me, back to my old flat. Maybe that's why Mr Dowling said they were taking me home.

We ease through Aldgate East Station. Lots of Pakistani zombies here. Dad would have hated it. I smile sadly. He was a wife-beating racist, but I'd be lying if I said I didn't miss him. He had his moments. There were sides to him that I loved and was proud of. Not enough to blind me to his faults though. I won't stand up for who he was and what he did. But still, he was my dad. He risked his life to help me. I'll happily call him a bigot and a bully, but if anyone else does, and I hear about it, they'd better watch out!

We're getting close to Whitechapel when the babies suddenly veer left. For a moment I think they've moved to avoid an oncoming train. But of course no trains run on these tracks now, and it's unlikely they ever will again.

There are scuffling noises. I can't see, but I think the babies are moving a panel aside. It takes a minute. Then the sounds stop and we start forward. The babies pause again when we pass through the opening into a new tunnel, to allow some of the pack to seal the entrance behind us.

'Intriguing,' I mutter. 'A hidden tunnel. I think we're getting close to our destination . . .'

As it turns out, I spoke too soon. By the occasional overhead light – they must be for the mutants – I see that we're in a network of low, narrow, roughly carved tunnels. I get the impression that these have been recently created, probably by the mutants or people who were working for them. It's even more of a maze than the sewers were. The tunnels branch off regularly, twist back on themselves, split up into sub-tunnels. I try keeping track of our route, but I'm lost after a couple of minutes. I actually get dizzy trying to keep up, and in the end I turn on my side and tune out.

Eventually, after maybe half an hour, we come to a green door. Eyeballs have been nailed or stuck to it, so that it seems as if the door is a multi-eyed creature casting its gaze over us. It blocks the tunnel completely, illuminated by an overhead lamp. One of the babies knocks on the door three times with a hammer which is lying nearby. It strikes one of the eyes on its second blow and the globe of liquid explodes in a sticky, messy geyser.

There's a short delay. The babies wait patiently. Then a voice crackles over an intercom unit which I can't see. 'Hit us with the password, sweet things.'

'*open sesame*,' the babies dutifully chant.

'And in whose name do you request entrance?' the guard asks.

'*the crimson clown's*,' the babies respond.

'Cool as ice cream,' the guard cackles.

Locks are turned. The door swings open. And a bowing mutant waves us in as we move forward, leaving the tunnels behind, to wend our way into the rancid bowels of Mr Dowling's demonic domain.

THREE

I'm expecting something outlandish and hellish, and Mr Dowling's base doesn't disappoint. It's an insane, weirdly colourful, chaotic place, the perfect home for a psychotic clown.

Very few of the rooms are regularly shaped. The ceilings and floors are uneven. There are usually five or six sides to each room. Doorways are clumsy holes cut in the walls, some far wider than necessary, others so narrow that we can only just squeeze through. Windows have been built into certain walls, but all they afford are views of carved stone.

Most of the rooms are large, more like caves than living quarters. The majority are lit by Christmas-tree lights which have all been set to flashing mode. In some of the rooms, Christmas songs blare out on ancient record players. No CD or MP3 players here. Poor Vinyl's dad would have approved.

The walls are a mix of reds and browns. I'm pretty sure that the vibrant red colours are streaks of fresh blood, while the duller reds and browns, judging by the smell, are the product of a mixture of dried blood and excrement. I'd like to think that the shit is an animal product, but I've a nasty suspicion that it's been supplied by Mr Dowling's mutants.

The grisly paint has been smeared across the walls randomly in places, but in others it's been carefully applied. Crude drawings of people, animals, eyes and swirling shapes. They all seem to have been done by the same hand. I'm guessing it's Mr Dowling's. I mean, if he was going to hire an artist-in-residence, surely he'd have gone for someone with more talent.

If the walls were only decorated with the revolting

paint, they'd be disturbing enough. But scores of body parts are pinned to them too. Hands, feet, noses, ears and more. Heads are jammed on spikes sticking out of the walls, and just about every corner features an intact corpse hanging from the ceiling. Some are in an advanced state of decay. Some are fresher. And some, I notice sickly when I spot one of the corpses struggling weakly, are still alive.

Machinery is mixed in with the body segments. Lots of different engine parts have been welded together with knives, saws and other weapons. I'm not sure if these are sculptures or implements of torture. If the latter, Dan-Dan would have had a blast here. Mr Dowling's array of instruments put the would-be sailor boy's tools to shame.

Some of the rooms contain sparkling costumes and props that seem to have come from a circus. Trapeze bars lean against the walls, ropes lie piled in corners, juggling pins are stacked on tables. A giant cannon dominates one room like a holy relic. It's not a real cannon, rather the sort that propels

human cannonballs through the air. I eye it uncertainly as we pass, wondering what foul use it might have been put to by its unhinged owner.

There are photographs too, of famous murderers, crime scenes, concentration camp victims. I spot mutants busily removing or defacing certain photos. I don't think much of that until one of them waves a photo at me, smiling proudly. The photo has been set on fire, but before the flames eat into it I catch sight of a familiar face — Dan-Dan. He must have been one of the stars of the grisly exhibition in the past, but he's fallen from favour and is now being swiftly erased from memory. I can't say I disapprove. Sometimes history *should* be rewritten.

Lots of mutants are milling around, resting on couches, playing, eating and drinking. I even spot a few going to the toilet. The toilets are set in the middle of the rooms, no stalls, in open view of everyone, and instead of toilet paper they use tongues that have been harvested from their victims. When I see that, I offer up a quick prayer of thanks for my nonfunctioning bowels.

A few of the creeps are sleeping, but not on beds — they hang from the ceiling in harnesses, looking similar to the strung-up corpses. Others are sharpening swords or loading guns. Weapons are everywhere, freely stacked, accessible to all.

I attract a few curious stares as I'm carried past by the babies, but nobody is shocked to see me. I think it takes a lot to faze anyone in this place.

The complex seems to spill on forever. The babies march me around for at least a quarter of an hour. Of course they might be doing repeat circuits to make it feel bigger than it is. The rooms all look the same after the first few. Each features such an array of head-spinning atrocities that they soon blend into one huge, migraine-inducing blur.

Finally we come to a room with a hearse in the centre. I don't know how they got it here. Maybe they took it apart, then rebuilt it underground. It gleams as if brand-new. No bloodstains or shitty smears on this morbid little beauty.

The babies stop in front of the hearse and set me down. As I stand, shivering and gawping, they quickly undress me. I don't protest. They leave my bandages intact, but remove everything else. When I'm naked, they pick me up again and hold me above their heads. I wait for them to do something, but they're like statues now.

My creepily cute carriers hold their pose for ages. They don't move. I lie still, not sure what they're waiting for, but enjoying the peace and quiet. No mutants enter the room. We're alone.

Finally the man of the hour, Mr Dowling, appears in all his gruesome glory. He hops into view, giggling ghoulishly, faithful mutant sidekick Kinslow close behind. He starts to undress as he comes towards me, kicks off his clown's shoes, then wriggles out of his pinstripe suit. He's not wearing anything underneath.

The flesh of his torso has been sliced away in many places, as it has been on his fingers, to reveal veins, arteries, bones, guts. Bolts have been driven into his ribcage in several places. Four pins have been stuck into his chest over his heart. Blood oozes slowly from the wounds.

I don't look at his groin. When I die, I don't want my last thought to be a recollection of Mr Dowling's dangly bits.

Kinslow strips too. The mutant's a real mess, like the rest of his kind. His skin is pustulent, purple in places, peeling away in others. Untidy grey hair. Yellow eyes. Teeth either black with rot or missing. No fingernails. A scabby, shrivelled tongue. Not the sort of beau you dream about taking back to meet your parents.

As the babies set me on my feet, so that I can face Mr Dowling directly, I mutter, 'There's far too much stripping going on for my liking.'

'Worried we're going to seduce you?' Kinslow chuckles.

'Not with that shrimp of a thing,' I tell him.

Kinslow glowers at me. I don't know if my jibe is justified or not – I haven't looked – but it seems to be a sore point.

'Seriously though,' I growl, my fingers balling up into fists. 'If either of you sickos makes a move on me . . .'

'Don't worry, Becky,' Kinslow says. 'This isn't a time for romance.'

'Then why have you taken your clothes off?' I ask.

'You'll find out in a minute,' he promises.

Mr Dowling leans towards me, until we're almost nose to nose, and beams as if he's been waiting all his life for this moment. The skin of his face is rippling. The v-shaped channels in his cheeks are bright pink, and gaps around his eyes where he's carved the flesh away are thick with soot — he must have touched them up on his way here.

'Hey, good-looking,' I croak, forcing a limp smile. 'What you got cooking?'

'You, if you're not careful,' Kinslow says, stepping up beside his master.

I sneer. 'You can't frighten me with talk like that. You wouldn't have brought me all this way just to stick me in a cannibal's pot.'

Kinslow laughs. 'You're mistaking us for logical creatures. We've done far stranger things than this, just for the hell of it.'

Mr Dowling makes a gurgling sound and Kinslow

nods obediently — he can read his mute master's thoughts, the way the babies can read mine. 'But you're right. We didn't bring you here to eat you. Though we're not ruling it out if you misbehave.'

The naked clown extends his arms and sighs deeply as he hugs me. I stiffen nervously, afraid that his fingers are going to wander, but he just holds me innocently, the way a child would hug its mother. I can feel his heart beating, fast and hard. As he pulls back, he opens his mouth to reveal a small snake slithering around his long, black tongue. He picks it out and drops it in the cavity where my heart should be. I squeal and tear the snake loose.

'Arsehole!' I snap at Mr Dowling. 'What did you do that for?'

'It was a gift,' Kinslow smiles.

'Tell him to get me chocolates next time.'

Mr Dowling snickers, then warbles something at the babies. They move to the side of the hearse. Kinslow opens the driver's door and the clown sits in. The mutant hurries to the passenger door and gets in too, sliding across to the middle of what is a single long seat.

The babies gently push me into the car after Kinslow and close the door on me. '*bye-bye mummy,*' they call. '*see you soon. we love you mummy.*'

'I love you too, little ones,' I laugh hysterically, blowing theatrical kisses after them. Most don't see, because they're already filing out of the room, but the baby with the hole in its head looks back at me solemnly, then bares its fangs in a quick smile and returns my wave.

I turn my attention to the pair in the hearse. They're both looking dead ahead, no pun intended. I glance over my shoulder. There's no coffin in the back.

'What now?' I ask but they don't answer. 'Is this what you guys do for fun of an evening?' I try again.

Kinslow winks. Then he presses a button in the dashboard. The seat starts to recline. Since the other two seem at ease, I lie back nervously and reluctantly go along with whatever's happening.

As the seat levels out, it also moves backwards and

the leg rest rises until we're lying flat in the back of the hearse. I start to think that maybe this is where the clown and his pet sleep, and they're turning in for the night. The thought that I'm sharing a glorified bed with Mr Dowling and his henchman doesn't do anything to settle my nerves.

'Are you sure you don't have any funny business in mind?' I croak.

'We're not predators,' Kinslow says haughtily. 'Not that kind anyway.'

'Well, you can't blame me for thinking the worst,' I tell him. 'Two naked guys invite a young lady into their hearse-styled bed . . .'

'Foolish girl,' Kinslow snaps.

'What have I done to get up your nose?' I frown.

'This isn't a bed,' he says.

'Then what is it?' I ask.

He flashes his blackened teeth at me. 'A portal to pleasures of the sweetest, most refreshing kind.'

As I'm trying to figure that one out, the seat beneath us suddenly splits in two and a void opens up. I shout with surprise and fear as we drop abruptly. I thrash wildly and open my mouth wide to scream.

But the scream's cut short when we splash into a vat of thick, slimy, sickly-sweet liquid. As I go under and twist around, I get a familiar taste and realise what I'm immersed in — *blood.*

FOUR

I come up in a panic and gasping for air. It's out of habit — my lungs don't work, so there's no fear that I might drown. As I bob up and down, I cast my gaze around. We're in a large chamber, a mix of bedroom, living room and laboratory. Once I have my bearings, I make for the edge of the vat, eager to scramble out of this nightmarish swamp.

'What's the rush?' Kinslow says.

I look back and spot the mutant floating on his back, arms crossed behind his head, as if we're in a swimming pool. Mr Dowling hasn't surfaced yet.

'What the hell is this?' I splutter.

'A literal bloodbath,' he chuckles, rolling round and dunking his head to take a deep swallow of the filthy soup.

As I stare at the back of Kinslow's head, Mr Dowling pops up out of the mess and spits a stream of blood into my face. I screech with outrage and throw a fist at him. That knocks me off balance and I go under again.

As I come up this time, I realise the vat isn't just filled with blood. There are objects floating in it. Grey, gooey chunks. I guess most people wouldn't recognise the gunk, but I've had plenty of experience where this substance is concerned and I place the bits instantly — brains.

'You can tuck into them if you want,' Kinslow says, sticking his head up out of the blood, 'but they're not particularly appetising. They add to the kick of the stew. Best just to stretch out and soak up the goodness.'

'What goodness?' I growl, but I'm already starting to feel better. The pain has ebbed and I'm not as exhausted as I was when the babies were holding me.

'This is our version of Oystein's Groove Tubes,' Kinslow explains as Mr Dowling dives to the bottom of the vat again. 'It's not as restorative as his syrup, but it kicks in more swiftly. Perfect when you need a shot in the arm.'

'It'll take more than a quick fix to sort me out,' I grunt.

'Don't be so sure of that,' Kinslow says. 'A dip in this once a day and you'll be bouncing about the place in no time.'

Sniffing dubiously, I swim to the edge of the vat and study my surroundings. The room is much the same as the others that I've seen, except with the addition of a bed, some large sofas and lots of laboratory equipment. There are also posters plastered across the walls, a mixture of childish drawings and photographs. The photos are all of two people, always shot separately, but pinned together in the posters. One of the subjects is Mr Dowling. The other is me.

I stare with unease at the photos. I don't mind the drawings – they're just the clown's clumsy handiwork – but the photos cover most of my life. There are shots of me when I was a baby, a young girl, a teenager. A few are recent, but most date back to before I became a zombie. I'm unaware of the photographer in all of them. These aren't photos that I posed for. They were taken when I wasn't looking, by sinister paparazzi who must have been trailing me for most of my living days.

'Where did he get all of these?' I ask quietly.

'He was keeping an eye on you,' Kinslow snickers.

'Why?'

The mutant shrugs. If he knows – and I'm sure by his sly smile that he does – he's not telling.

Mr Dowling surfaces again beside me, points to a photo that looks like it was taken on my first day at school and makes a whining noise.

'He says that's his favourite picture,' Kinslow trans-lates. 'He wishes he could have walked you to school that day. He would've loved to have slaughtered all of the other children as a present for you, so that you'd have known how special you were.'

'I bet he never got booked for many children's parties,' I mumble, feeling sick and confused at the thought of having had this monster trailing me for all those years.

Mr Dowling turns his gaze on me, his eyes dancing more feverishly than usual in their sockets. He doesn't make any sounds, but he must be communicating telepathically with the mutant, because Kinslow starts supplying words for him again.

'He's sorry he couldn't take you from your school ahead of the attack. He sent me along to keep an eye on you, but I was under orders not to rescue you or show favouritism. You had to come here as an equal, of your own free will. He wasn't sure you'd revitalise, or even if you'd survive at all, but he had faith. He says that ultimately we must all cling to belief and hope for the best.'

'That day in the Imperial War Museum,' I mutter, thinking back. 'You were there to test me, weren't you? It wasn't the baby you were after. You came to check on me, to see what I'd do in a situation like that.'

Kinslow nods. 'We knew the day of reckoning was almost upon us. Mr Dowling wanted to find out what you were made of, if you had what it would take to pull through. He was worried about you. Knowing how positively you reacted in an emergency helped set his mind at rest.'

'But why?' I whisper. 'What's so different about me? Why does he care? Why has he been shadowing me for so long?'

Mr Dowling shakes his head softly. He reaches up and runs a blood-drenched finger across my left cheek, drawing some sort of a pattern on it. Then he runs the fingertip across the tops of my severed ears. I wince but he doesn't withdraw. Instead he gurgles something.

'We've soaked up enough nutrients,' Kinslow says. 'It's time.'

'Time for what?' I squint.

Kinslow swims across like a shark until his face looms large in front of mine and grins with sadistic relish. 'Time to build a new Becky Smith,' he purrs.

FIVE

We climb out of the vat and Mr Dowling races across the room to the lab equipment. He doesn't dry himself off, so he leaves sticky red footprints in his wake. Kinslow and I follow at a more casual pace. Then Kinslow pauses to pick up a robe lying on the floor and pull it on.

'Is there one of those for me?' I ask.

'You're fine as you are,' he says.

'Get me a damn robe or I'll fight you for yours,' I growl.

Kinslow rolls his eyes, but nips behind the vat and

49

find another robe, which he passes to me. I struggle to slip it on – the worst of the pain has eased, though it flares up again if I move about too much – but eventually I'm able to tie it shut and I follow Kinslow, hobbling slightly. I'm still in a lot of pain, but it's nowhere near as excruciating as it was a few minutes ago.

'That's strong stuff,' I note, rubbing some of the liquid between my fingers and then over my lips.

'It's even more effective if you're half-alive like me,' Kinslow grins. 'I feel like I'm wired to the national grid.'

'The blood doesn't play much of a role in the mix, does it?' I ask.

'Clever girl,' Kinslow coos. 'Yeah, it's there for colour and taste more than anything else. It's not entirely decorative – it adds an element that would be hard to replicate otherwise – but hardly essential.'

I gaze down at the exposed sections of my arms and legs. I'm like a life-sized red jelly baby. 'Can I wash this off?' I ask.

'No,' Kinslow says. 'There isn't time. Besides, Mr Dowling prefers you this way. He loves a bit of a mess.'

The clown has headed for what looks like a dentist's chair. Ignoring the fact that he's as red and sticky as me, he pulls on a green gown and a white mask as we approach, rolls on a pair of surgical gloves, then changes his mind and peels one of them off. He motions for me to advance.

'What's he going to do to me?' I ask Kinslow, reluctant to place myself in the hands of a homicidal maniac after having so recently slipped through the fingers of another.

'Don't worry,' Kinslow says. 'I'd be lying if I said this wasn't going to hurt, but he wants to help. We can't let you stagger around in your current condition. Your guts will rot, your muscles will atrophy, your brain will curdle, you'll be in agony all the time. To save you, we need to turn you into a new young woman.'

'I liked the old version,' I moan.

'He did too,' Kinslow says. 'But Lord Wood

destroyed you. It's up to Mr Dowling to restore what has been ruined.'

I eye the dentist's chair suspiciously, but what choice do I have? I'm in the clown's lair, deep underground, surrounded by enemies who could rip me apart in the twinkling of an eye. I'm in no position to make demands or refuse commands. With a groan, I climb into the chair and lie back.

Mr Dowling produces a pair of handcuffs and taps the arms of the chair.

'What the hell?' I shout, bolting upright.

'They're only to hold you in place while he's working on you,' Kinslow says soothingly. 'Leather straps would be better, but he prefers cuffs. You don't have to let him chain you down – we won't force you – but this is going to last a lot longer if we have to stop every time you squirm. And believe me, you *will* squirm.'

'You'd never have made a nurse,' I grumble. 'No bedside manner.'

He shrugs and Mr Dowling jangles the handcuffs.

'I really don't feel comfortable with this,' I whisper.

'It's like a scene from a horror flick. Two guys lure the pretty heroine into their den, then tie her down and ...'

'You're not that pretty,' Kinslow cackles, and laughs even harder when I shoot him the finger. Then he sobers up. 'We're not going to do anything nasty to you. We're trying to help you, Becky. Refuse the cuffs if you want, but you'll regret it if you do.'

I think it over, almost tell the clown to stuff the cuffs, but then decide to gamble. Grumbling away darkly to myself, I lie back, slam my arms down on the rests and let Mr Dowling cuff them. He then ties down my legs using a length of thick rope.

'That's got heavy-duty wire running through it,' Kinslow tells me. 'It will hold firm no matter how much you struggle.'

'That's a relief,' I say sarcastically.

He turns to Mr Dowling. 'Where do you want to begin, boss?' The clown considers it, then squeaks and points at my midriff. 'Right,' Kinslow says, producing a large pair of scissors. 'This isn't going to hurt ...' He cackles like a witch. '... *us!*'

Leaning forward, he undoes my robe. I curse him and tell him to leave it as it is, but he ignores me. I start to panic, thinking that I've misread the situation, that Mr Dowling and Kinslow *are* just a pair of dirty old men. But it quickly becomes apparent that neither of them has any lurid interest in my body. They're studying me with purely clinical expressions.

Kinslow crooks his neck from left to right, to work out any kinks, then starts cutting the bandages away from around my ribs, and I brace myself for the torment that's about to begin afresh. But at least this time there's going to be something positive at the end of it all. Or so I want to believe.

SIX

Once Kinslow has cut through all the bandages, he pulls them out from beneath me and dumps them in a large bin set a few metres back from the chair. Mr Dowling bends over to peer into the mess of my stomach. Dan-Dan peeled away the surrounding flesh and snapped off most of my ribs, leaving only stumps at the sides.

'What's it like in there?' I ask Kinslow as he returns and studies the contents of my exposed stomach. When he doesn't answer, I try raising my head to look.

'Don't.' Kinslow stops me with a rare show of sympathy. 'You don't want to see this. Trust me.'

I lean back again and moan. It's times like this that I wish I could cry.

Mr Dowling reaches into the cavity and pulls something out. Maybe it's my liver or a kidney. He nibbles on it, laughs, then tosses it at the bin. It misses and skids across the floor. The clown doesn't seem to care. He roots around and looks for other organs to remove.

He works on my stomach for ages, yanking bits out, scraping other areas clean. Sometimes he sews stuff together.

In a few instances, he inserts tubes and wires, connecting whatever he thinks needs to be connected.

It doesn't hurt as much as when Dan-Dan was breaking through my ribcage, but I'm far from comfortable. I jerk and wince a lot, occasionally cry out with genuine pain.

'Can't you give me a bloody anaesthetic?' I snarl at Kinslow.

'They don't work on zombies,' he says. Mr Dowling

mutters something and Kinslow nods. 'Besides, you're being born again here, and birth should be painful. It's part of the charm.'

'Typical men,' I sneer. 'My mum always said that if men had to give birth, painkillers would have been invented centuries earlier than they were.'

Mr Dowling ignores my protestations and pushes on. I whimper, shriek and swear, but I might as well be whistling nursery rhymes for all the attention he pays.

He spends a long time testing my lungs. Although our lungs don't work the way they do in the living – we've no real need of them – our revitalised brains force them to operate to a limited extent, drawing air down our throats and then pumping it back up, allowing us to retain the gift of speech.

'He's concerned,' Kinslow says as Mr Dowling goes off looking for something. 'Your lungs have been severely damaged and they'll continue to deteriorate. He's going to insert a small pump in your throat. He developed it himself. It'll mean you no longer have to rely on your lungs when you're talking.'

'Whatever,' I sniff.

The clown returns and manoeuvres the pump into place. It's a brief, painless procedure. But then he starts to remove my lungs.

'Stop!' I cry, my voice sounding slightly different, but nothing too noticeable.

'What's wrong?' Kinslow asks.

'I don't want him to take out my lungs. What if I need them some day?'

'You won't. The pump will last as long as you do.'

'Even so, surely I need them for balance, or to fill the space, or . . .'

Kinslow squints at me. 'Are you a biologist?'

'Of course not.'

'Then leave this to those who know better,' he says, and Mr Dowling carries on over my objections, ridding my body of the lungs which I once relied on for life, dumping them on the floor for me to stare at glumly.

When he finishes with my insides, he heads off for a break. Kinslow pulls the robe closed over my sting-ing body, dips a sponge in the vat of blood and brains, then squeezes it over my face.

'Don't swallow,' he says as I open my mouth. 'Mr

Dowling has rejigged your digestive system. It'll work better than it did before – vomiting won't be as difficult or unpleasant as it was – but it'll be for the best if you don't ingest anything for a few days, to let all the joins seal properly.'

'He should have rejigged my lungs too while he was at it,' I grumble, still mad at the clown for what I'm sure was unnecessary overkill.

'Don't you ever quit complaining?' Kinslow snaps.

'Well,' I grin savagely, 'my dad used to say I'd stop when I died, but obviously he was wrong.'

Mr Dowling returns with a box of metal parts and a welder's torch. As I watch warily, he pulls open my robe and screws metal spikes into the stumps of my ribs. When they're all in place, he picks a large, rib-shaped metal rod out of the box and fires up the torch.

'Is he sure he knows what he's doing?' I ask nervously.

'Eighty per cent,' Kinslow cackles. Mr Dowling corrects him with a tut. 'Well, maybe seventy . . .'

The heat from the torch on the remains of my ribs causes me to scream with all my might. I feel like my insides are on fire. I beg the clown to stop, but he calmly moves on from one rib to the next, until the entire set has been welded into place.

'That wasn't too bad, was it?' Kinslow asks with fake concern when Mr Dowling finally turns off the torch and steps back to assess his work.

I can't respond. I'm gasping like a dying fish, eyes wide. I still feel like I'm on fire.

'I'd toss a bucket of water over you,' Kinslow says, 'but it might interfere with the machinery that Mr Dowling put in earlier. Don't worry. You'll feel right as rain in no time.'

As the metal ribs start to cool, Mr Dowling works swiftly. He trots off again and this time returns with a bucket full of scraps of human flesh. Digging out a lengthy piece, he begins stitching it to the skin at the side of my ribs.

'This is all taken from zombies, in case you were worried that we'd harvested it from living humans,' Kinslow says as I moan wordlessly, trying to make the clown stop. 'It's not that he objects to the use of living flesh – you know him better than that – but their skin wouldn't mesh with yours. Living flesh needs fresh blood to sustain it.'

'What about *my* blood?' I ask weakly, my voice having returned as the heat faded. 'I lost a hell of a lot of it when Dan-Dan was working me over. Are you going to give me a transfusion?'

'No point,' Kinslow says. 'Undead bodies reject the blood of others, whether it's from someone living or a zombie. You wouldn't gain any benefits from it. The blood would simply slosh around inside you.'

'Will my body ever replace the blood that it's lost?'

'No, but you don't need it. Your body will adjust and find ways to work without it. You won't be quite as fast or sharp as you were before, but you'll be able to function in more or less the same way.'

The flesh that Mr Dowling stitches across my steel ribs comes from all sorts of people, white, black, Asian. Some chunks are smooth as leather, others as hairy as a gorilla's armpit. I look like a patchwork quilt when he's finished. I hate it, but the clown nods happily and claps with delight.

'He thinks that's his best job yet,' Kinslow tells me.

'Does this often, does he?' I growl.

Kinslow winks. 'Let's just say you're not the first.'

Having given me a new stomach, Mr Dowling spends ages looking at my chest, particularly at the area where my right breast used to be. He takes all sorts of measurements before disappearing for half an hour. He returns with a perfectly formed but slightly oversized boob.

'That's a bit bigger than what I'm used to,' I note icily.

'He knows,' Kinslow says, 'but he thinks it will fit better, given all the other work that's been done to that area. You don't mind, do you?'

I shrug. 'No. If it was a lot bigger, I'd have an issue, but that one's all right. Is he going to stick a matching breast on the other side?'

'No,' Kinslow says.

'I suppose it would cause complications if he covered the gap where my heart used to be?'

'No,' Kinslow says. 'But that hole is a part of you now. He thinks you'd be denying who you truly were if you tried to cover it up.'

In a weird sort of way, I can see where he's coming from. I find it hard to remember what I was like without the hole in my chest. As horrified as I was by it in the early days, now I think I'd miss it if the clown filled it in.

Mr Dowling focuses on my fingers and toes once he's sewn the breast into place. After another trip to wherever he stores these things, he screws replacement bones into the tips of each digit until I have a full set, like I did before Dan-Dan ripped them out and ground them down.

'These won't be as effective as your original bones,' Kinslow says. 'Don't rely on them as much as you normally would. For instance, I wouldn't recommend trying to dig them into a brick wall.'

'Will the original bones grow back?' I ask.

'Eventually, yes, but it'll take time. We'll monitor your progress and remove the extensions when appropriate, although they'll snap off sooner or later if we leave them.'

The clown-turned-surgeon doesn't do much with my arms and legs. There are gaping wounds running up them where Dan-Dan sliced, gouged and drilled, but Mr Dowling doesn't seem worried about those. He stitches a couple of the larger holes, but leaves the rest as they are.

Finished with my torso and limbs, he closes the robe, then turns to my head and starts to get artistic. Dan-Dan hammered nails into my skull. He was careful not to pierce my brain, so the clown could easily pull them out without causing any damage, but he doesn't even try. Instead he uses them as posts to weave a crown of wire around. I argue with him – what the hell do I want with a crown? – but he just gurgles and carries on.

Next he attaches metal, elf-like ears to the side of my head, cutting away the bits of ear that Dan-Dan left behind.

'Looking good, Tinkerbell,' Kinslow giggles.

'Get stuffed,' I growl. 'I'll rip these idiotic things off as soon as my hands are free.' But it's an idle threat. I hate the look of the ears – Mr Dowling holds up a mirror for me – but my sense of hearing has improved dramatically, even better than it was before Dan-Dan snipped away my natural pair.

My cheeks were sliced apart by the child-killer. Mr Dowling puts in a few stitches at the edges to stop them widening any further, then starts painting the exposed flesh with a variety of colours.

'Stop that,' I yell. 'I'll look like a bloody rainbow.'

But, as usual, he turns a deaf ear to my outraged cries, applying his paints with a serious expression, like Timothy Jackson at work on one of his zombie drawings.

Next he focuses on my eyes. Dan-Dan didn't do anything to them, but the clown tuts and goes to a fridge, returning with a small jar.

'What's in that?' I ask nervously.

'Contact lenses,' Kinslow says as Mr Dowling takes one out and leans towards me with it finely balanced on a finger.

'Hold it,' I yelp, jerking my head aside. 'Dr Oystein said we couldn't wear contact lenses, that they'd scratch our dry eyes and damage our sight.'

'Normal contact lenses would,' Kinslow agrees.

'But these are special. Your friend Owl Man invented them. They have a sensitive coating that allows your lot to endure them. You can leave them in all day and night. Each pair will last around a month.'

'You're sure they won't scratch my eyeballs?' I ask, letting Mr Dowling widen my eyelids and slip the first one in.

'Well,' Kinslow smiles, 'about sixty per cent sure . . .'

Finally Mr Dowling examines my mouth and attaches steel heads to the teeth which were filed down. Then he screws in fake fangs, filling the gaps where other teeth were extracted. They hurt like a bitch going into my gums. I'd have bitten through his fingers except he inserted a clamp before he went to work.

'The teeth are more complicated than your fingers and toes,' Kinslow says as Mr Dowling removes the clamp. 'Your natural fangs will grow again over time. The caps will stunt their growth and sting every day until they're removed, but there's no way round that if you want a fully functioning set of gnashers right now. We'll keep a close eye on the implants and detach them as soon as we can.'

'You're too kind,' I snarl, running my tongue round my new teeth. They feel smoother than the others.

Kinslow returns to the vat, soaks the sponge again and squeezes it over my face, chest, stomach, arms and legs. He does that a few more times, coating me in the icky substance. The robe is as red and sticky as the rest of me now. I probably would have been better off without it, though I'm not going to admit as much to Kinslow.

'Can't you just let me crawl back into the vat?' I ask.

'A dip a day is enough,' Kinslow says. 'Besides, we're not done with you yet. There's one more thing we need to tend to before we let you go.'

'What?' I frown, doing a quick inventory of my body parts, wondering what they might have missed.

'Did you ever read *Frankenstein*?' Kinslow asks.

'No.'

'But you must have seen some of the movies?'

'Of course, numbnuts. I didn't live in a cave.'

'Good. Then you'll know what was needed to bring the monster to life.' As I stare at him uncertainly, he picks up a cable from the floor, waves it in front of my nose and sings with wicked relish, *'E-lec-tric-i-teeeeee!'*

SEVEN

'Hold on a minute!' I yelp as Kinslow plugs the cable into a socket. There's a long metallic wand attached to the other end. 'What are you doing?'

'This is going to hurt a *lot*,' Kinslow says, examining the tip of the wand, then pressing a switch in the handle. It makes a weird buzzing noise. Kinslow grunts and turns it off, then hands the wand to Mr Dowling.

'So you brought me here to torture me,' I snarl. 'You're the same as Dan-Dan.'

'Not at all,' Kinslow protests. 'This is something everyone who is close to Mr Dowling has had to endure. I've been where you are. I've felt your pain. Literally.'

'I don't understand!' I shout as Mr Dowling flicks the switch.

'You will soon,' Kinslow whispers.

Then Mr Dowling touches the wand to my forehead and the world crackles madly around me. My back arches. My mouth and eyes shoot wide open. I spasm out of control. Vision and hearing fade. Everything goes white. The buzzing noise fills my head. It's like I'm falling into a pit of vibrating nothingness. I lose all sense of spatial awareness.

After a timeless time, somebody finds me in the middle of the void and gently murmurs my name. '*Becky.*' A pause. '*I love you, Becky.*'

At first I think it's the babies. But although this voice is similar, it's not the same. It's deeper, without the hollow ring that the babies have when they speak.

'Who are you?' I ask, though I'm not sure if I ask it out loud or inside my head. 'Where am I?'

'*In my arms, where you always should have been. You know me, my dove. I do not have to name myself.*'

74

'Mr Dowling?' I say hesitantly.

'*Who else?*'

An image of the clown materialises in front of me. But he's not naked or in his costume. Instead he's clad in a white suit. He has normal hair and eyes, and his skin doesn't ripple.

'This isn't real,' I moan.

'*Of course it is,*' he says. '*I mean, it's only happening inside our heads, but that doesn't make it any less real.*'

He reaches out and I sense him caressing my cheek, even though I can't see my own body in this realm.

'*I wish I could speak to you like this all the time, but my body is not entirely mine any more, and hasn't been for a long time. I can't complain. It suits my purposes to wear the form of a madman in the physical world. It makes my difficult task so much easier than it would otherwise be. But it does get in the way of communication, there's no denying that.*'

'Is this what you used to look like?' I ask, studying the man in front of me, his white suit almost invisible against the white background.

'*I don't know,*' he smiles. '*I can't remember. But you can find out if you wish.*'

'What do you mean?'

For a few seconds nothing happens. Then I get a flood of images, memories from Mr Dowling's past, of him studying his reflection in a variety of mirrors. There are other memories too, idyllic recollections of a woman who might have been his wife and sweet-mannered children who look like they were his. But they're quickly followed by atrocious scenes of him killing people, filling his mouth with insects, carving the v-shaped channels in his face.

'Stop,' I moan. 'I don't want to see inside your head.'

'*But you must,*' he says softly. '*Just as I must see inside yours. Ours needs to be a complete union. Bodies, minds, souls.*'

'What are you ranting about now?' I huff, trying to push myself away from him, failing because that's hard to do when you don't have an actual body.

'*The reason I have brought you here,*' he says. '*The reason I kept tabs on you since you were a baby. The* reason I helped you whenever I could since you became a revitalised.'

'And?' I ask when he pauses.

There's silence for a while. Then he sighs. '*You have only seen me at my worst. I don't blame you for being wary of me. I have given you little in which you can trust. But know this, Becky Smith, and believe it — I love you.*'

I gawp at him, astonished. I can't think of anything to say in the face of such a ridiculous proclamation.

'*I want you to pledge yourself to me,*' he continues. '*It will be a beautiful ceremony, the wedding of the century. Afterwards you will be mine and I will be yours. Mr and Mrs Dowling. The happy couple I always hoped we would be.*'

I laugh in his face, finding my voice again. 'You always were a loopy son of a bitch,' I jeer, 'but now you've lost your marbles entirely. What the hell makes you think I'd want anything to do with a crazy, murderous creep like you?'

'*It's your destiny,*' he smiles, not offended by my outburst.

'Bullshit,' I reply. 'I'll make my own destiny,

thanks very much, and there's no room for you in it, not unless I'm slitting your throat and ripping out your heart.'

Mr Dowling shakes his head and chuckles. '*So fiery. I adore that about you. I need people with your spirit. Our children will prosper under your firm influence when our minds are fully joined.*'

'*Children?*' I splutter. 'You seem to be forgetting something, wacko. I'm one of the walking dead, so I'm all dried up inside. I can't have kids.'

Mr Dowling shrugs. '*You have a point. We might one day find a way around that obstacle, but even if we don't, we can always adopt.*'

'Not interested,' I sniff. Then I scowl. 'What do you mean, *when our minds are fully joined*? Aren't they joined now?'

'*This is only the first connection of many,*' Mr Dowling says. '*My brain operates on a variety of levels. This is the most basic. I grant access to this level to all of those who carry out my bidding, since it allows us to communicate directly. Others, such as Kinslow, enjoy access to higher levels, allowing them insights into my more personal mental spheres. Only you will be granted full, all-areas access, once you have seen the light and freely offered yourself to me.'*

'I'm honoured,' I drawl sarcastically.

'*You will be,*' he says seriously.

Then the white haze starts to fade. The real world rematerialises. Mr Dowling is slumped beside me, limbs twitching, as are mine. He must have pressed the wand to his own head after zapping me. As the pair of us whimper and slowly start to recover the use of our bodies, he pushes himself away. I spot Kinslow nearby, clothed. He's fetched clothes for us too, a circus outfit for the clown, normal gear for me.

Mr Dowling opens his eyes – they're rolling wildly again – and smiles. He puts a couple of shaky fingers inside his mouth, roots around and produces a small key, which he unlocks the handcuffs with. Then he loosens the ropes around my legs. Leaving me to free myself, he starts to dress.

'I'm glad that psycho's out of my head,' I mutter to Kinslow as he passes me jeans, a T-shirt and a pair of trainers.

'*But I'm not,*' Mr Dowling whispers inside my skull. With a yelp, I drop the clothes and glare at the clown. '*Why are you surprised? I told you this was how I communicated. Once we have joined, the link cannot be broken. I will always be able to speak to you from this day forward.*'

'I preferred it when you were mute,' I mutter.

'*That is unfortunate,*' he says sweetly without turning to look at me. '*Because I will never be mute for you again.*'

'Can you hear that too?' I ask Kinslow as I get rid of the robe and pull on the clothes, trying to ignore the fact that I'm still caked with blood and tiny scraps of brain from the vat.

'No,' he says. 'Mr Dowling can address a group if he chooses, but most of the time he operates on a one-to-one basis.'

'You'll never guess what the lunatic said to me,' I snort. 'He wants me to be his wife and rear his children.'

'Well,' Kinslow says, 'that *is* why we went to all the trouble of rescuing you.'

My smile fades. 'You're serious? That monster really does want to marry me? I thought he was just messing with my mind.'

'Don't think of him as a monster,' Kinslow says, pulling a disapproving expression. 'Think of him more as a . . . groom.'

As Kinslow cackles, Mr Dowling pulls on his over-sized shoes and clicks his heels together. '*Come*,' he says inside my head. '*Let me take you on a short tour.*'

'Where?' I ask.

'*My den*,' he says, choosing the word deliberately.

'Why?' I press.

'*To explain why, of all the women in the world, my heart can belong only to you.*'

'You know, if you keep saying stuff like that, I'm gonna start thinking you're reading from a slushy movie script,' I tell him.

'*I read only the lines that you have written in the fabric of my soul*,' he says in response, then laughs when I make a gagging gesture. '*Enough of our games, Becky. I know that you crave answers, and it's time I supplied you with some. Will you take my arm?*'

'No,' I say gruffly as he extends his right hand towards me.

'*As you wish.*' He looks sad for a moment, but then he beams brightly. '*But I'll bet any amount you care to wager that, by the end of your stay here, you'll take my arm gladly.*'

'In your dreams, weirdo,' I huff.

'*Yes,*' he nods. '*This is a world of dreams.*'

He sets off ahead of me. Kinslow pokes me in my newly installed ribs when I don't instantly follow. I might be the mutant's mistress-in-waiting, but for the time being it looks like I'm to be treated to no more freedom than a slave. Fair enough. I'm used to that. It doesn't bother me in the slightest. Let them think they have me exactly where they want me. Others have thought that way before, until I've taught them not to mess with the B.

Groaning, I shake my arms to loosen them up – I can still feel the electric current buzzing through me – then limp after the marching clown … the insane killer … my self-proclaimed husband-to-be.

EIGHT

There's a spiral staircase hidden away in one corner of the room, leading up to the hub of the underground den.

'Why didn't we come this way instead of splashing down into the vat of blood?' I ask.

'It's more fun entering via the hearse,' Kinslow grins. 'We're all about the entertainment factor here.'

Mr Dowling leads me on a tour of the complex. He bounds along with the excitement and energy of a puppy going for a walk. He stops frequently to mingle with his mutants, pat their heads, clap their backs, join in if they're playing games. At one point he even pauses by a large, fat man who is taking a crap, waits until he's finished, then – and this is an image I hope to banish from my memory banks as swiftly as I can – wipes the giggling mutant's bum with one of the human tongues that they use for such functions!

'That's going *way* above and beyond the call of duty,' I moan to Kinslow.

'A touch on the extreme side perhaps,' Kinslow snickers. 'Then again, the world might have been a better place if the leaders of the past had made a point of wiping a few of their voters' backsides every now and then. It brings the mighty and the meek together.'

'*Friends, Romans, countrymen, lend me your arses,*' Mr Dowling trills telepathically, and I have to laugh.

Images from the clown's brain keep flicking through my head. It's like catching glimpses of a photo album or reality TV show through blinds which keep opening and closing without warning. Most of it's mundane, flashes of him swimming, playing with his children, cavorting with his mutants, prancing through the streets of London. But at one stage I get a picture of him leaning over a test tube, studying a milky-white liquid. I can't be sure, but I think this is Schlesinger-10, the virus which could wipe out the whole of humanity if released.

The image vanishes as swiftly as it formed. I can't bring it back, but I pay more attention from that point on. It would be a major coup if I could find out where Mr Dowling is storing his stolen sample of Schlesinger-10 and somehow get word back to Dr Oystein.

Most of the rooms are familiar from when the babies were escorting me to Mr Dowling's personal chambers. But one place I haven't seen before is a massive laboratory, tucked away behind a system of sealed doors. There are dozens of scientists and nurses at work. Some toil at lab equipment and computers, but others are experimenting on humans and mutants.

'This is where we were born,' Kinslow says, smiling nostalgically. 'The first few generations of mutants were created elsewhere, in labs around the world, but Mr Dowling has based himself in London for the last twenty years. Virtually all of us with him now started off our new lives here.'

'Are they volunteers or slaves?' I ask, nodding at the subjects. Some seem happy enough, but others are shuddering and screaming into gags.

'A mix,' he says. 'Most of the mutants are here voluntarily. Mr Dowling and his team are finding ways to fine-tune our forms all the time, but they need guinea pigs to work on. The majority of his loyal followers are willing to step forward when asked. A few have been dragged here against their wishes, if the scientists need a specific type of person to run a test on and nobody matching their requirements raises a hand. But the bulk have come because they want to.'

'And the humans?'

Kinslow shrugs. 'Many are specimens we've captured, but others chose to take part. They want to join our ranks and they accept this as the price they must pay.'

'*Specimens*,' I sneer. 'That's how the soldiers and

scientists referred to zombies in the complex where I was held when I first recovered consciousness.'

Kinslow shrugs. 'What can I say? It's a big, bad world. At least we don't pretend to be the good guys. What you see is what you get with us.'

'How come *he* isn't telling me all this?' I ask, nodding at Mr Dowling as he trots off to check on one of his more unwilling subjects. 'He's hardly said a word since we left his digs.'

Kinslow sighs. 'Our leader is a man of few words. It's not easy for him, focusing his thoughts. His brain is immense, with many things running through it at the same time. You'll realise that when he grants you access to the higher levels. At any one moment he might be agonising over a dozen complex formulas, while analysing data from experiments that took place years ago, and considering various chess moves.'

'Chess?' I frown.

'He's a big fan. He's studied games by all the grand masters. He replays them and looks for moves that the masters missed. Refinement is second nature to him. He's always looking to improve.

'It's chaos in that wild, wonderful head of his,' Kinslow continues sadly. 'Any ordinary person would be mentally crushed beneath the weight of what he deals with every day. You or I would be a vegetable if we had to process even a fraction of what he does in any given hour.

'It's taken its toll. The madness isn't an act, but he can overcome it to a limited extent when he needs to. Externally he's a mess – he lost control over his body years ago – but internally he can drag himself down to our level, or close enough so that he can address us in a way that we can comprehend.'

'You're trying to paint him as a tragic figure?' I snort.

Kinslow glares at me. 'There's nothing tragic about Mr Dowling. He sacrificed his sanity gladly. He's the greatest genius this world has ever seen. You should be proud that he considers you worthy of his attention and time.'

'I'd rather he didn't pay me a blind bit of notice,' I sniff.

'That's why you're an uncouth young lady,'

Kinslow snarls. Then he smiles. 'But Mr Dowling will educate you and raise you up in the world. He won't dismiss you as a lost cause, even though anyone else in his position would.'

'Tell him not to do me any favours,' I mutter, faking a yawn, and I love it when Kinslow bristles and shoots me evils.

The tour continues. The rest of the rooms seem uninteresting after the lab, until we come to the nursery. I know that's what it is because the word is painted in blood, in large letters, over the door. I expect Mr Dowling to say something at this point, but he just pushes in as if it's the same as all the other rooms.

There are several sections to the nursery. We first enter a room full of cribs, all sorts of designs and sizes. Most are vacant, though I spot a few of the fanged, white-eyed, pint-sized monstrosities at rest. Their mouths move softly as I pass, each of them whispering the same word, '*mummy*.'

The next room is full of toys. Soft dolls, beautifully carved houses, replicas of cars and guns, model planes hanging from the ceiling, mobiles, carousels, inflatables, jigsaw puzzles, board games. It's like an Aladdin's cave for very young children.

'Stunning, isn't it?' Kinslow says.

'There's too much,' I croak, head spinning as I look around. 'I can't take it all in. The babies must go wild in here.'

'Actually they've no interest in toys. Mr Dowling put the collection together because he thinks it would be good for the babies to play, but they ignore every toy he's ever brought. That distresses him. He wants them to have fun, but their brains don't work that way and he hasn't been able to refocus them, as hard as he's tried.'

'Well, that's the trouble with breeding a crop of savage rug rats,' I murmur.

Kinslow nods glumly. 'He keeps trying to introduce an element of play into their genetic code, but I doubt he'll succeed. They're a solemn bunch.'

'He should have let them hang out with Dan-Dan,' I say sourly. 'There was a killer who knew all about *play*.'

We push through a door into a classroom. Scores of the eerie babies are sitting in rows round a teacher, staring at her expressionlessly as she holds up large pictures for them.

'Repeat after me,' the teacher says. 'A is for apple.'

'*a is for apple*,' they whisper.

She puts the picture aside and picks up another. 'A is for ape.'

'*a is for ape*.'

She nods and picks up a picture of a killing field, bodies ripped apart, guts everywhere, blood soaking into the ground. 'A is for atrocity,' she sings.

'*a is for atrocity*,' the babies repeat.

'Very good,' she purrs.

I stare at the teacher with shock. It's not the pictures which stun me, or the way she holds the attention of the little monsters so artfully. It's the fact that I recognise her, that I've sat in a classroom with her before and had her lecture me in much the same way as she's now dealing with the babies.

Nudging forward, I raise a hand as if asking a question in class in the old days. (Not that I asked

many questions back then.) The teacher appraises me coolly, then purses her lips and nods.

'Yes, Miss Smith?' she gurgles, her voice deeper and more cracked than it used to be. 'Can I help you?'

I clear my throat, lower my hand, gawp at the teacher for another few seconds, then wheeze incredulously, '*Mrs Reed?*'

NINE

The last time I saw my old principal, Mrs Reed, she was tucking into the brain of another of my teachers. I've hardly considered her since then, although, now that I cast my thoughts back, I remember being confused because she was eating brains even though she wasn't a zombie. Now it's clear she was on her way to bigger and better things.

Ironically, when I met Vinyl in Hammersmith before we headed for New Kirkham, he suggested the possibility that she might have got a job teaching zombies, but he was only joking. Looks like the joke was on him in the end.

Mrs Reed's silver hair looks much the same as always, and she's wearing her customary black cape and thin-rimmed glasses. But her skin is mottled, purple in places. Her eyes are a dull yellow colour. Her teeth are black and some have fallen out, along with her fingernails. She's a mutant like Kinslow.

'You'd started to turn on the morning of the zombie attack,' I mutter.

'Yes,' she says primly. 'I had been informed of the plan to unleash the zombie virus and I chose that day to commit myself completely to Mr Dowling's cause.'

'You guys have to eat brains too?' I ask, looking from her to Kinslow.

'They're not as essential to us as they are to your kind,' Kinslow answers. 'But yeah, we have to top up every so often to keep body and soul together.' He touches a bit of loose flesh on his right cheek and pushes it back into place. 'I know we look bad, but we'd be a hell of a lot worse if we abstained from brains.'

I stare at Mrs Reed and she arches an eyebrow at me. 'Say what is on your mind, Miss Smith.'

'You were in league with them all along,' I accuse her. 'You knew what was going to happen. You let zombies invade our school and slaughter your students.'

'I did what I felt was right,' she says calmly. 'I have no regrets.'

'We wanted someone there to observe you,' Kinslow explains. 'We've had an operative at every school you ever attended.'

'Looks like you can't trust anyone these days,' I growl. 'I thought you'd have been happier in Battersea Power Station, that you'd throw in your lot with Vicky Wedge and her bigoted crowd.'

Mrs Reed tuts. 'Don't be dense, girl. That was a charade.'

I stare at her with surprise. 'You're not a racist?'

'Certainly not. I acted that way in order to get closer to your father and thus to you. He was a vile creature. I hope he got what was coming to him when the zombies ran riot.'

'Don't slag off my dad, you mutant bitch,' I snap. 'He was twice the person you were. At least he didn't feed a load of kids who were under his care to zombies.'

'Those children meant nothing to me,' Mrs Reed says, unfazed by my outburst. 'Fodder for the undead. Unimportant in the grand scheme of things. These were the only children I ever cared about.'

She looks at the babies and smiles. They're all staring at her as they were when I first came in. They haven't even glanced at me.

'Lynne has been invaluable,' Kinslow says. 'She has an amazing bond with the babies. They won't pay attention to most teachers, but they like her.'

'No,' Mrs Reed corrects him. 'They respect me.'

Mr Dowling glides forward, cruising through the ranks of babies, stroking their heads and beaming at them. Each looks up when touched and smiles briefly at him, then returns its attention to the teacher.

The clown's voice echoes in my head as he addresses the infants. '*Good babies. Who loves you?*'

'*you do daddy,*' they reply.

'*And Mummy,*' he tells them. '*Mummy loves you too.*'

'*mummy?*' the children whisper.

'B is for ball,' Mrs Reed chants.

'*b is for ball,*' they instantly reply.

'B is for beach.'

'*b is for beach.*'

'And B is for . . . Becky Smith!' she finishes with a flourish, waving an arm at me like a magician producing a rabbit.

Every baby's head snaps round and their tiny, eerie faces light up. '*mummy,*' they croon. '*you came to see us mummy. we love you mummy. sit with us. stay with us forever.*'

The baby with the hole in its head, the one from Timothy's place on Brick Lane, gets up and races across. I can't see its feet beneath its gown. It stops just ahead of me and holds up both arms. '*a is for apple mummy,*' it says proudly.

'Yeah,' I grunt. 'And A is for my arse, which you can all kiss if you think I'm going to stay and play mother to a pack of clay-faced freaks.'

The baby stares at me blankly.

'We will not have language like that in my class,' Mrs Reed thunders.

'What are you gonna do about it?' I jeer. 'Make me sit on the naughty step?'

My ex-principal advances angrily and raises a hand to slap me. Before she can, the babies leap to their feet, their eyes glowing a dark red colour. They snarl at her, showing their fangs, and bunch together between her and me.

Mrs Reed draws to a startled halt and her jaw drops.

'Withdraw, Lynne,' Kinslow advises her quietly. 'We won't be able to stop them if they attack.'

'They've never threatened me before,' Mrs Reed bleats, taking a trembling step away from me and lowering her arm. 'They're my students. They respect me. We have a close relationship.'

'Yeah,' Kinslow says, 'but they're B's children. You know what they say about blood being thicker than –'

'They're not my bloody children,' I shout. 'Why

do you keep saying that these horrible, vicious freaks are mine?'

'Because they are,' someone murmurs behind me.

And I turn to find myself facing the bulging pot belly of the towering, smirking, bug-eyed Owl Man.

TEN

'I should have known you'd turn up like a bad smell sooner or later,' I sneer.

'Becky,' he says, pulling a pained expression. 'Surely you could come up with something more cutting than that old cliché.'

'You're not worth the effort of an original put-down,' I sniff, and look for his sidekicks, Sakarias and Rage, but he seems to be alone. 'Where's your dog and the big galoot?'

'I left them with Dan-Dan's darlings,' Owl Man

says. 'I thought you might appreciate it if they guided the traumatised children to safety.'

I make a growling noise, then force myself to spit out a very spiteful, 'Thanks.'

Mr Dowling and Kinslow aren't surprised to see Owl Man, but I am. I knew he was working with the clown in one capacity or another, but I didn't think they were on such good terms that he could waltz into Mr Dowling's secret base any time he pleased.

'Will you ask the babies to sit?' Owl Man purrs. 'I think they're close to ripping Mrs Reed limb from limb.'

I cast my gaze over the babies. Their eyes are still glowing red and they haven't retracted their fangs.

'Maybe I want them to tear her apart,' I murmur, enjoying the way she stiffens fearfully.

'It makes no difference to me,' Owl Man says with a careless shrug, moving to the front of the classroom and leaning against the old-style desk.

'Can't Mr Dowling call them off?' I ask.

'Of course,' Owl Man says. 'But he seems happy to cede authority to you in this instance.'

It's true. The clown barely seems to have acknowledged Owl Man's presence or Mrs Reed's predicament. He's studying a map of the world, head cocked sideways, prodding a finger at different countries, as if trying to figure out where we are.

'It's OK,' I tell the babies, relenting. 'The old bat is harmless. Let her be.'

'*b*,' the babies echo, taking their places again, eyes fading from red to white. '*b is for bat. b is for becky smith. b is for mummy.*'

'Less of it,' I mutter, then sit among the babies. The one with the hole in its head nestles up to me and I pull it close like a doll. I know it was responsible for Timothy's death, but I don't think there was any deliberate malice in what it did. Timothy found it with a spike sticking through its head. It must have been in agony, maybe terrified, assuming these strange creatures can feel terror. When I pulled out the spike, it called for the zombies because it needed help and was lonely and scared, not because it wanted to kill my friend.

Or so I like to think.

'The clown promised me answers,' I tell Owl Man. 'I'm guessing you've come to supply them.'

'I certainly can if that is what he wishes.' Owl Man looks to Mr Dowling for confirmation. The clown gives no outward sign that he's paying attention, but he must transmit something mentally, because Owl Man nods. 'Very well. And you are happy for me to speak in front of the teacher?'

This time Mr Dowling does look round. He stares at Mrs Reed as if seeing her for the first time, then his voice comes to me inside my head. '*Will I kill her for you, Becky?*'

'No,' I answer quickly. 'There's no need to do that.'

Mrs Reed trembles as she realises that her life is hanging in the balance. Mr Dowling stares at her a moment longer, then waves a dismissive hand and returns his attention to the map.

'If you'll pardon me a while . . .' Mrs Reed says weakly and hurries from the room, pausing only to shoot me daggers before she exits, blaming me for the aggressive actions of Mr Dowling and the babies.

'I'm glad you spared her,' Kinslow says. 'She'd have been hard to replace.'

'Oh, I'm all for supporting the educational system,' I say drily, then gaze at the grinning Owl Man. 'Go on. Enlighten me. I can tell you're dying to.'

Owl Man pats his pot belly and burps softly. 'Pardon me. I ate before I came, and food often repeats on me.'

'Like I give a damn about your feeding habits,' I huff. 'The babies. Tell me.'

'Your wish is my command,' he says, rubbing his stomach. 'The children are mutants, but a far more advanced breed than Kinslow or Mrs Reed. They have been cloned, not transformed. Unlike the regular mutants, who started out as normal people, these have been born as they are.

'They're remarkable creatures,' he continues as the babies stare at him the way they were staring at Mrs Reed when she was teaching. 'A miracle of modern genetics. Zombies and mutants are Neanderthals in comparison with these state-of-the-art creations. The babies are the foot soldiers of the next generation, the crop we dreamt of harvesting when we started down this long, ungodly road years ago.

'I'm not sure how much Oystein has told you about our working history, but the three of us were once a team.'

'I know about you and the doc,' I interrupt. 'He told me you were his star assistant until you betrayed him and made off with a sample of Schlesinger-10. But who's the third member?'

Owl Man blinks with surprise. 'Why, Mr Dowling of course.'

I gawp at him. 'You're lying.'

'Why would I lie?' he counters.

'Dr Oystein would never have worked with a foul monster like *that*,' I growl, stabbing a finger at Mr Dowling, who takes no notice of the insult. He's moved on from the map and is now thoughtfully chewing a piece of chalk.

'He wasn't always this way,' Owl Man says, studying the chalk-chewing clown with what appears to be genuine pity. 'He's a genius, and there was a time when he could control himself the way you and I can.'

'The doc thinks he's the servant of Satan,' I snap.

'He does now,' Owl Man nods. 'And, for all I know, he might be correct. But there was a time when he trusted Mr Dowling even more than he trusted me. The three of us made giant strides together. I was always the most junior of the trio, but I had a way of slotting neatly between the other two, translating their more theoretical ideas into workable practice.

'I won't bore you with the break-up of the partnership. Oystein has his side of the story, I have mine, and I'm sure Mr Dowling has his, though he has never shared the complete tale with me. However it happened, relations shattered and we parted company acrimoniously. I have restored certain confidences over the years, as you can see by my presence here, but I doubt we'll ever share as much as we did when we were younger and pulling in the exact same direction.'

'Interesting that you decided to go with the evil

lunatic rather than the kindly doctor,' I sneer. 'You showed your true colours in the end, didn't you?'

'That is how some might see it,' Owl Man says evenly. 'For my part . . .' He tuts. 'But we need not venture down that path. I have no interest in earning your favourable opinion. Let's focus on the babies.

'Mr Dowling was always more interested in the mutant gene than the zombie virus. Oystein was fixated on the undead, but Mr Dowling was intrigued by the inbetween state. Each of the scientists aided the other in his research, while I divided my time equally between the pair.

'All three of us were involved in the early development of the babies. They captured Oystein's eye because they had the capacity to serve as an army in the war with the zombies. If we could not manufacture a virus that was capable of wiping out the undead menace, maybe we could use a semi-living force to take the battle to them.'

'Couldn't you have used regular mutants?' I ask.

'Oystein didn't trust them,' Owl Man says. 'He thought they might form a splinter group and act against the best interests of humanity, try to gain control of the planet for themselves.'

'As they have,' I say smugly. 'The doc had these creeps sussed from the very beginning.'

'Careful,' Kinslow says roughly. 'I might put you over my knee and spank you if you keep offending me.'

'Not while I have my babies to protect me,' I smirk.

Kinslow's eyes narrow but he says nothing more. He seems to be worried that the babies would actually take my side over his if push came to shove. I file that nugget away. It might come in handy when I'm trying to blow this joint later.

'We made a number of early advances,' Owl Man continues. 'We hadn't yet bred any babies, but we were not far off. Then the schism opened between us and our research on that front had to be abandoned while we retreated, recovered and regrouped.

'When Mr Dowling returned to the matter of the babies years later, it became clear to him that they would need to be cloned. He experimented on a number of fertilised human eggs, but –'

'Pick those up at the local supermarket, did he?' I interject.

'Actually you'd get a nasty shock if I told you where they came from,' Owl Man says. 'But that's a story for another day.'

'There seem to be lots of those,' I mutter.

'More than you could imagine,' Owl Man says darkly. 'Now, as I was saying, Mr Dowling conducted experiments on ordinary human embryos, without success. The mutant gene always ran amuck, destroying the developing beings. He needed to add something to the mix to combat the effects of the mutant material, but he couldn't figure out what it was.'

'Let me guess your next words — *then it struck him.*'

'Then it struck him,' Owl Man grins. 'The vaccine that Oystein had developed, which allowed certain people to revitalise. Maybe *that* would do the trick.'

'So he broke into the doc's lab and hijacked a case?' I guess.

'Yes,' Owl Man says. 'But it didn't work. He

exhausted his supply on a variety of tests and got nowhere. He went back to the drawing board and concluded that he needed a sample of the vaccine which had passed through a person's system. He could have stolen another case and injected his own guinea pigs, but there seemed little point when it would be easier to take blood from a selection of the thousands of infants being processed by Oystein's operatives every year.'

'Wait a minute,' I wheeze, seeing where this is headed. 'Stop.'

'He targeted a hundred children,' Owl Man continues as if I hadn't spoken. 'He did it furtively, without alerting Oystein or any of his team. Alas, no joy. Every experiment that he conducted with their blood was a failure. But he had a feeling that he was on the right track, so he tried another hundred.

'Nobody knew – or knows – why certain people have the ability to revitalise. There was no way of telling which of Oystein's subjects might recover the use of their brain after they'd been turned into a zombie. So he decided that he needed to keep on going until he found the blood of one with the . . . shall we say, *right stuff*?'

'No,' I croak, pushing aside the baby with the hole in its head and lurching to my feet. 'You're making this up to freak me out.'

'He got lucky with his second hundred specimens,' Owl Man purrs. 'Judging by the results when he injected their blood into the embryos, six of the children had whatever was genetically required to combat the zombie gene. If he had shared his results with Oystein, it might have enabled the doctor to fast-track his vaccination programme and identify the people who were viable candidates for revitalisation. Thousands of lives could have been saved. Unfortunately Mr Dowling has had no desire to aid the doctor in any area since they went their separate ways, and he cares nothing for the well-being of ordinary mortals. Humans are playthings to him.

'Anyway, Mr Dowling found himself the proud owner of six fertilised, healthy, zombie-resistant embryos. It would have made sense to hatch all six, but he was worried that if he created several breeds, they might fight with one another, as humans of different races have done since the dawn of mankind. He wanted only one of his precious crop.

'He and I were back on speaking terms by that stage,' Owl Man says, ignoring me as I numbly shake my head. 'He involved me in the choice, as he felt that would bring us closer together. I arranged for him to visit all six of the children whose blood we had utilised. They were young, some of them little more than babies themselves.

'Mr Dowling studied each child, probed their senses, tried to determine their character. I'm not sure he knew exactly what he was looking for, but he certainly recognised it when he found it. One of the children impressed him more than the others. A feisty little girl. He decided to keep the baby which he had created using *her* blood.'

'No,' I whisper again.

'He destroyed the other five embryos and sat on the sixth like a mother hen,' Owl Man goes on. 'It took longer than he thought, almost three years, but finally it hatched, a beautiful, genderless mutant,

which didn't rely on brains to survive. Mr Dowling declared himself well pleased, and immediately set about making many clones of the baby. Cloning is something both he and Oystein mastered decades ago, though Oystein never pursued it himself.

'Every baby here is a clone of that first specimen. They are all the offspring of that original girl, the one Mr Dowling chose to be the mother of the future.

'Now, you're a bright young thing,' Owl Man concludes with sadistic relish. 'Do I need to tell you the girl's name, or have you figured it out already?'

In answer, I can only stare at him, then down at the babies, hundreds of horrors, each one the product of Mr Dowling's brilliant but twisted coupling with . . . *me*.

ELEVEN

'*we love you mummy.*' That's what the babies whispered in my nightmares when I was alive and capable of sleep. I thought they were mocking me. I never guessed they were expressing genuine affection, that they truly saw me as their mother.

'Wait,' I mumble, sitting down again. 'The dreams. Why did I dream about the babies? I never saw any of this lot before that day in Brick Lane.'

'They have a telepathic link with you,' Owl Man says. 'We're not sure how or why. I was astonished when I learnt about your nightmares. I wished to bring you in for closer study, but Mr Dowling insisted you be left to your own devices.'

'He's always been soft on you,' Kinslow snorts.

'*It is not softness*,' Mr Dowling whispers inside my head. '*It is love.*'

I ignore the clown and stay focused on Owl Man.

'The babies instinctively knew of their attachment to you,' he says. 'They recognised your face when we showed them photographs of you. Some would occasionally sneak out and shadow you. We were worried that they would try to make contact, but they never approached you. They simply wanted to watch you go about your day-to-day life. Maybe they were reassuring themselves that you were in good shape.'

'If they liked me that much, why did they always kill me in my dreams?' I grunt.

'I think *you* contributed the more nightmarish elements,' Owl Man says.

'What's that supposed to mean?' I frown.

'I'm not a psychoanalyst, but it seems likely to me that you knew about the babies on a subconscious level. Part of you realised that they regarded you as their mother, that you might one day be forced to bear responsibility for them. I think you demonised them in your dreams in an effort to sever your link with them, to deny what destiny seemed to have in store for you.'

'If I had that much control over what I dreamt, why didn't I give myself the power to kill them off in my nightmares?' I ask.

'You were afraid,' he says. 'You didn't understand what was happening to you. This was your developing brain's way of trying to deal with the issues at hand.'

'Bloody brains,' I grumble. 'They've caused us nothing but hassle since we evolved away from apes. We should have stayed in the trees. We'd have all been happier and a hell of a lot better off.'

'Perhaps,' Owl Man nods. 'But this is where we find ourselves. And now you know where the babies came from, why you dreamt about them and why Mr Dowling has wanted to reunite with you ever since.'

'Actually I'm not so sure of that last one.' I look at

the clown. He has put the chalk aside – or swallowed it – and is staring at me, eyes rolling every which way at once. 'So you used my blood to create and clone the babies. Big deal. My part in this should have finished there. Why come looking for me years later?'

'*Because I love you,*' Mr Dowling croons.

'Stop saying that!' I glare.

'*But it's true.*' He comes towards me, arms waving wildly, spitting out bits of chalk. '*I knew it the first time I explored your mind. You and the babies are my world. I love you all and want you around me as we press forward. We will be a family. I'll find peace again in your arms.*'

'The only thing you'll find in my arms is a big butcher's knife, which I'll bury between your shoulder blades the first chance I get,' I tell him.

The clown giggles and starts hopping around. '*Mr Dowling and Becky, sitting in a tree, k-i-s-s-i-n-g!*' he sings.

'Are you getting any of this?' I ask Owl Man with disgust.

'Not at the moment,' he smiles. 'But I can guess

what he's saying. He really does love you. That's evident to us all.'

I pull a disgusted face. 'Yeah, well, it's the love of a lunatic. I'm sure celebrity stalkers used to think they were truly in love with their prey, and that the people they were bothering would love them in return. But I've no interest in this sick creep. I'd rather get it on with Kinslow — don't take that as an invite,' I add as the mutant theatrically brushes back his hair and smiles.

'*But you must love me,*' Mr Dowling says, sounding confused. '*We're meant for one another. I've built a kingdom for you. These are your babies. We need you.*'

'Tough,' I snap. 'You repulse me. I wouldn't pledge myself to you if you were the last man on earth. Hell will freeze over before you'll get even a kiss on the cheek from me, Romeo.'

Mr Dowling cocks his head and studies me gloomily. He seems genuinely taken aback by my rejection, unsure how to react.

'Let's not be hasty,' Kinslow mutters uneasily.

'Don't say anything in the heat of the moment that you might regret later.'

'Get stuffed,' I tell him, then focus on Owl Man. 'You can't expect me to go along with this. If you've been keeping tabs on me all this time, you know me better than that, don't you?'

'Yes,' he says. 'But I also know how persuasive Mr Dowling can be. If I was a gambler, I'd bet on you succumbing to his charms in the end, Becky.'

'It's B, numbnuts,' I jeer. 'B Smith, plain and simple, and I plan to keep it that way. I'm not in the marrying frame of mind. You'll have to look for a lover elsewhere, clown.'

Mr Dowling's eyes close for a moment. When he opens them again, there are tears of blood in both corners.

'*don't cry daddy,*' the babies wail, crowding closer to hug his legs and stroke him soothingly.

In response, the clown points a finger at me and the babies snap round, the way they did when Mrs Reed threatened me. I think he plans to set them on me and I get ready to fight to the death. But when he makes a gesture with his right hand, they simply swarm forward, pick me up and hold me over their heads as they did when they first brought me underground.

'*If you won't love me of your own free will, then you leave me with only one option,*' Mr Dowling hisses inside my head, leaning forward to eyeball me.

'Torture?' I guess, glumly resigned to another bout of suffering.

'*No, silly,*' the clown laughs, then kisses his fingers and presses them to the crown that he wove for me. '*I will have to woo you!*'

TWELVE

The babies cart me through the complex, Mr Dowling lolloping along behind, Kinslow and Owl Man bringing up the rear. He bombards me with scenes from some of his favourite romantic films as we proceed – most are ancient black-and-white weepies – along with spliced images of the pair of us, beaming like the happy couples in the movie clips.

I doggedly ignore the clown's mental feed, arms crossed, face like a slapped arse. I'm not amused by his advances. I'm glad my friends from the old days aren't around to see me humiliated like this. I'd have been a laughing stock if this had happened in front of Vinyl, Trev and the rest.

I'm taken back to Mr Dowling's personal quarters. This time he doesn't bother with the hearse, and the babies set me down by the top of the stairs. I descend in silence with the clown, Kinslow and Owl Man. As soon as we clear the steps, Mr Dowling heads for his lab, clicking his fingers for Kinslow to accompany him.

'I really think you should keep an open mind,' Owl Man murmurs as we wait for the clown to return.

'Not a hope,' I snort. 'He's a madman. A killer. Evil to the bone. I have no plans to marry, but if I did I like to think I could do better than *that*.'

'You have killed too,' Owl Man reminds me. 'You shouldn't be so quick to judge.'

'I've done bad things,' I admit, 'but there's a world of difference between me and that wacko. I'm offended that you think we're one and the same.'

Owl Man sighs. 'That's not what I said. I was simply pointing out that you have both endured dark times and lashed out in savage ways. Mr Dowling is a confused, tormented soul. He's not vile as Dan-Dan was. Lord Wood chose to pursue his twisted path, whereas Mr Dowling is a victim of circumstance.'

'Bullshit,' I spit. 'I don't care what he's been through. We all have a choice.'

'Not if we've been stripped of our rationality,' Owl Man argues. 'When you were a revived, you slaughtered indiscriminately and ate the brains of those you killed. I don't hold you responsible for your actions, because you were nothing more than an animal acting as your nature dictated.

'Mr Dowling is in much the same state as you were then. He cannot control his base urges. He interprets the world as a random, wild, vicious place and reacts accordingly. In his disturbed frame of mind, he sees nothing untoward in the way he behaves. In a world of the insane, insanity is the logical response — that's how he comprehends it.'

I shake my head stubbornly. 'Save your breath. You'll never convince me. He can communicate normally with me when he speaks inside my head, so he must know what's right and wrong.'

'That is why he's such a tragic figure,' Owl Man says. 'A good man still exists inside him, but that man is trapped. He cannot take control of his body the way you or I can. He's a victim.'

'That's a feeble excuse. He could regain control if he wanted, if he forced himself to focus. It's just easier this way, waltzing through life not giving a damn. He isn't trapped. He's hiding.'

Owl Man glares at me. He starts to say something, then stops and grimaces. 'I really wish you would trust me, Becky — I mean, *B*.'

'Why should I?' I counter.

Owl Man considers that, then nods glumly. 'Point conceded. Very well. I see that my words are falling on deaf ears – and such pretty new ears they are – so I will leave you in the care of your intended. As I said earlier, I'm sure he'll win you over in the end. Don't despise yourself when you renege on your promise to keep him at arm's length.'

'Where are you off to?' I ask, strangely sorry that

he's leaving. At least I can have a proper conversation with the owl-eyed freak. I don't like the idea of having only Mr Dowling and Kinslow to chat with.

'I'm going to find Sakarias and Rage,' Owl Man tells me.

'Watch out for that one,' I snort. 'He'll turn on you eventually, like he did with Dr Oystein.'

'I know,' Owl Man says. 'But sometimes we must go into partnership with those we'd prefer to distance ourselves from. It's the way of the world. If I was to interact only with the people I truly trust, I'd hardly deal with anyone at all.' He pauses, then says sincerely, 'You would be one of the few.'

'You old flatterer,' I grin. 'Why don't you bump off Mr Dowling and take me with you? I wouldn't mind bringing *you* a cup of hot chocolate and your slippers at night.'

Owl Man laughs. 'If I thought you were serious . . .' He smiles warmly. 'Good luck, B. Take care. We'll meet again, I'm sure, and, when we do, perhaps we can form a mutually beneficial partnership of our own.'

On that odd note he takes his leave. I stare after him as he climbs the stairs. I don't know why, but there's something about the weirdo that I'm starting to warm to. He's in league with the bad guys, but I get the sense that in his own way he's trying to do good. I just don't see how he thinks he can achieve anything positive by siding with Mr Dowling and his beastly crew.

Before I can pursue the notion any further, someone taps my shoulder. I look round and find Mr Dowling standing behind me. He's holding the wand that he shocked me with earlier.

'*Darling*,' he whispers, then presses the wand to my forehead and sends me shooting off into a world of electrical sparks and spasms.

THIRTEEN

It soon becomes apparent that this is Mr Dowling's idea of courtship. He doesn't bother with poems, flowers or chocolates — for him it's all about electrocution and sharing his twisted thoughts with me.

As my senses go into shock and I lie thrashing on the floor, the clown zaps his own brain and pulls me further into his strange, hallucinogenic mind. He opens up to me, revealing large chunks of his early life, memories of him with his wife and children, at work, reading, swimming. He loved to swim when he was human. He lived in a place where it always snowed heavily in winter, but regardless of that he'd swim in lakes and rivers all year round.

Judging by the style of clothes that I spot in his flashbacks, he's older than I thought. Then again, it's hard to judge the accuracy of his recollections. Things get muddled. I'll be watching him and his wife sitting by an old-style radio, listening to the news, when suddenly a spiky-haired punk will wander by the window, arm in arm with someone wearing a *Vote For Obama* T-shirt.

If Mr Dowling is out walking as a young man, the cars that he spots are mostly vintage, but there are modern models mixed in with them, even a few electric cars.

Most of the memories play up his sympathetic, human side. I see him all loving and caring with his family, volunteering in a hospital, helping out in a home for the elderly. There are images of him walking away from people who are taunting him for one reason or another, turning his back on violence. At one point he picks up a dead dog which has been run over and cries softly.

'Yeah,' I sneer. 'You'll cry for a dog, but what about all the people you've killed?'

'*That's different,*' Mr Dowling says. He's wearing the same style suit as when he projected himself into my head earlier, but it's blue now, not white. '*This has become a world of the dead. People don't matter any more. It's hell on earth. We might as well revel in the chaos while we can.*'

'That's why you're a monster,' I snarl. 'You've given up on people and treat them like scum. I never will. It doesn't matter how bad things get, we should never lower ourselves to that level.'

He stares at me uncertainly, apparently troubled by my words. But then the vision fades and I find myself returning to reality, moaning weakly on the floor, the clown hopping around, giggling insanely, poking me with a severed arm while Kinslow looks on wearily.

The pair carry me over to the vat of blood and brains. Kinslow tries to undress me, but I snap at him that I can do it myself. He starts to argue, but Mr Dowling must have a word, because he stops and makes a *whatever* gesture. Wriggling out of my clothes, I crawl into the vat to soak. Mr Dowling checks that I'm OK, then heads up the stairs with Kinslow, off to deal with whatever today's mad business entails.

I'm weary after my tour of the complex, so I relax and soak up nutrients for a while. When I'm feeling sprightlier, I slip out of the vat and shuffle across the floor, not worrying about the stains I'm leaving behind — the floor's already covered with old blood smears, so a few more won't make any difference. I climb the stairs, only to find the door at the top locked. I return to the room and go on a circuit, giving it a full sweep, looking for ways out.

I find a shower hidden behind a screen in one corner, which cheers me up no end – I don't want to have to crawl around covered in blood and muck every day – but there are no obvious exits. This seems to be a sealed chamber. I'm sure it isn't – I can't believe that Mr Dowling would box himself in with no way out if he ever came under attack – but if there are secret doorways, they're too cunningly hidden for me to locate, at least in my current subdued state.

I have a look at the area above the vat, thinking I might be able to climb out through the hearse, but the walls are smooth, solid steel. Too high for me to jump. I could build a pyramid out of furniture, but I doubt I'd be able to break through the covering at the top. It's steel, the same as the walls, and Mr Dowling doesn't strike me as someone who overlooks the minor details.

I limp across to the lab and study the implements which are lying out in open view. Knives, saws, drills, needles, Bunsen burners. I could tool up, lie in wait for Mr Dowling, attack when he returns.

But he's surely anticipating that. I'd be swatted like a fly. Better to leave these for the time being. Maybe strike at him later, when he's not expecting it. Play along, pretend to fall for him, wait for him to lower his defences, then . . .

I pick up a knife, smiling grimly at the thought of slitting the clown's throat. The smile fades as I realise I could slit mine instead. Well, no, that wouldn't put me out of action. But I could pound it through my skull, dig it into my brain, free myself from Mr

Dowling's influence, escape this whole stinking cesspit of a world.

I stand there for ages, toying with the idea, wondering if this is the moment for me to clock out.

In the end, I turn my back on the darkness. The thought of Dr Oystein stays my hand. The doc wouldn't give up, not when there's so much of the game to be played. He'd hang tough, watch things develop, wait for his chance to round on the clown. The doc would never have abandoned me to the mercy of his most bitter enemy, but now that I've fallen into Mr Dowling's clutches, it could be a golden opportunity to strike a fatal blow.

I have to be careful. The clown might have left orders for his sample of Schlesinger-10 to be released if he's killed. I must not attack him until I'm sure it's safe, that Kinslow won't wipe out the remnants of humanity in retaliation. But the option is on the table. If I removed myself from the equation, that chance would be taken away. This isn't my time to die, not while I might still be of use to Dr Oystein.

Reluctantly I set down the knife, shuffle back across the cave, climb into the vat and float in the crimson goo, soaking up goodness, feeling slivers of my vitality return, thinking, plotting, waiting.

FOURTEEN

The *great courtship* continues in much the same way as it started. Mr Dowling doesn't spend much time with me, but pays a visit every day, hits the pair of us with his boom-boom stick, then slips inside the eye of my mind while we're writhing uncontrollably on the floor.

The details he shares have become more intimate. I'm also able to probe his thoughts to an extent now, and access memories of my choosing. For instance, if I want to see more of his family, I can spend a session tapping into that particular part of his brain and watch him cuddling his wife or playing games with his children, reading bedtime stories to his three daughters, swinging his son around in the air.

There are limits to how far I can probe. Whenever I try to find out where he might be storing his Schlesinger-10 sample, the curtains come crashing down and I get redirected. Still, as he opens up further to me, I keep on digging. It will be hard for him, as he reveals so much about himself, to guard his privacy from every angle. I might be able to slide in on the sly one day and find something which I can use against him.

I must admit, I've started to feel sorry for the psychotic clown. Owl Man was right when he said that Mr Dowling was a tragic figure. If his memories are to be believed, he was a man of dignity once. He loved his family. He helped out in the community. He was charitable.

What turned his world upside down and left him in this mad, tempestuous state? I try to figure him out, but he always steers me away from those memories. There are almost no images of Dr Oystein or

Owl Man that I can access. No footage of the respectable Mr Dowling losing his mind, coming undone, donning the clown's outfit for the first time.

It's like he's split his life in three. He'll share old memories with me, the good times, his normal life. And he's happy for me to see him in his current shambolic condition. But he's cut out the middle section, his fall from grace. Maybe he's deliberately hiding it from me, or maybe he's buried it so deep that even he can't access it. Perhaps those memories are too painful for him to face again.

I have to remind myself, when I feel pity building within me, that he's a killer, a sadist, a loose cannon who can strike at anyone, any time. It doesn't matter that he was once a good man, if fate dealt him a horrible hand. Right now he's the greatest threat this world has ever faced, with the power to wipe out every living person. I can feel sorry for him later, if I find a way to overcome him. Until then I have to look for chinks in his armour and do all in my power to chip away at them.

When I complain about being bored, he lets me

out of his private chambers a few times to visit the babies. Kinslow and some of the other mutants always tag along to escort me, then wait outside the nursery, guarding the exit in case I make a break for freedom.

The babies like it when I sit with them. I join in their lessons and help Mrs Reed teach them, though they get distracted easily when I'm there. I can tell she'd rather I stayed away, but she can't say anything in case I order the babies to attack her.

I learn a lot about the tiny terrors during the course of our time together. For instance, I already knew they weren't reliant on brains for nourishment, but I find out that they hardly need to eat anything. Each of them can go weeks, even months without feeding or drinking.

They don't excrete as humans do. Their bodies break down the waste into liquid and they sweat it all out. I thought that was gross when Mrs Reed explained it to me, and I avoided cuddling up close to the infants for a while, but I've adjusted to the idea and it doesn't bother me now.

The baby with the hole in its head always waddles up close to me when I sit down with them. I feel more of a connection to that one than the others. The rest all look the same. At least I can tell Holy Moly apart. (I know — stupid name! But it suits the little monster and it was the best I could come up with.)

'Do they have individual personalities?' I ask Mrs Reed one day.

'Not that I'm aware of,' she says. 'They blend together in their lessons. I've tried isolating individuals – I made a few wear name tags of my choosing, and taught them separately from the others – but they consistently thwart my efforts. If one of them learns something, they all learn it. They share everything telepathically.'

'Holy Moly is different though, isn't it?' I note. 'The others don't come up to me every time.'

'How can you be sure?' she counters. 'Several slip up close to you whenever you visit. Perhaps they're always the same, and the one with the hole in its cranium just happens to be among those assigned the task of personally guarding you.'

I stare at the babies, wondering if they have secret names for one another, if they see tiny differences in each other that we're unaware of.

'It's not the same as our old school, is it?' I mutter.

'I prefer the set-up here,' Mrs Reed sniffs. 'At least my students pay attention now.'

I asked her about my classmates during an earlier visit. A few of my friends escaped with my dad on the day of the zombie apocalypse and I'd love to know if they got out of London, or if they ran out of luck in the end, like poor Vinyl. But she couldn't tell me anything.

'You were the only pupil I cared about,' she said. 'I had no interest in the rest of the unruly, ignorant mob.'

I rub Holy Moly's head, ignoring the ever-present temptation to stick a finger into the hole in the baby's skull. I've tried having conversations with Holy Moly and some of the others, with limited success. They'll sometimes answer basic questions, but more often than not they'll simply respond with their familiar croons.

'we love you mummy.'

'stay with us mummy.'

'we want to hold you forever.'

'Why do you do this?' I ask Mrs Reed. 'Why betray the human race in favour of Mr Dowling and his mutants?'

'Long life is one reason,' she says after a moment's pause. 'We don't live anywhere near as long as your kind, but I could last a few hundred years if I'm lucky. And Mr Dowling might find a way to extend that even further.'

'But who wants to live that long in a hellhole like this?' I grunt.

'Lots of us evidently,' she says curtly. 'There's also the appeal of reshaping the future. When Mr Dowling's people convinced me that the end of the world was coming, I saw a chance to contribute to the creation of its replacement. These are monumental times. When the history books are written, I'll have a place in them as one of the architects of the new society.'

'A society of mutants,' I drawl. 'Big deal.'

'It will be,' she says. 'These babies are only the first generation. Think what our ancient ancestors must have been like when they crawled out of their caves, rough, brute creatures. The descendants of these infants will go much further than we ever did.'

I frown. 'You think the babies will be able to reproduce?'

'Of course not,' she snorts. 'They have no sexual organs. But they can be cloned, and we – or they – will find ways to improve upon what we've already created.'

'You reckon there could be some budding scientists among this lot?' I smile.

'Certainly,' she says. 'It's hard to judge their IQ since they're so introverted, but we're fairly sure they're more intelligent than we are. We should be able to get a clearer idea as they age. We think they'll become more open with us as they mature.'

'How long will that take?' I ask.

'They should hit adolescence within seventy years,' she says. 'Full adulthood will come forty or fifty years after that, along with the ability to tap into the staggering potential which Mr Dowling has imbued them with — he has designed them to have control of many more areas of their brains than we do.

'Don't you see, Becky?' she beams. 'We've been given a chance to play God. Who could walk away from the opportunity to sculpt the world as they see fit, to guide the early steps of a whole new civilisation?'

'What was wrong with the old bunch?' I growl.

'Small-minded animals,' she says dismissively. 'Mankind had plenty of time to change but we didn't. Wars, hatred and bigotry were our legacy. Forgive me if I show our people no allegiance, but I would rather focus on those with genuine promise.'

'Judas,' I sneer.

'Do you think so?' She smiles icily. 'According to the Bible, Judas betrayed the son of God. Who have I betrayed? Thugs, polluters, warmongers, killers, wife-beaters, crooked politicians, thieving bankers, splintered family units, the blank-eyed TV generation, children who could only connect to the world via a computer.'

'Mr Dowling is a crazy killer,' I point out bitterly.

'Yes,' she says, 'but he will pass. We all will. Our stain will be wiped clean eventually. My hope is that once we're gone a kinder race can evolve peacefully, achieve more than we ever did, be capable of getting more from – and doing more for – the world than we ever could.'

'Nothing can come of violence except more violence,' I argue.

'The Big Bang was the most violent moment in the history of the universe,' she counters, 'and look at everything good that came out of that.'

'That's hardly a fair comparison,' I note.

'Maybe not,' she sighs, 'but I live in hope. I know we're evil individuals, but we're products of an evil society. I believe we can only make a clean break with the past by ridding ourselves of the baggage that has weighed down the human race for so long. Perhaps I'm deluded, and the babies will turn out even worse than their creators, but I've gambled everything – my soul included – on the hope that good *can* spring from the ashes of wickedness.

'And that is why I pledged myself to Mr Dowling,' she concludes as I stare at her mutely, confused by what she's said. 'So tell me, Miss Smith, do I still seem like a cold-hearted monster to you now?'

FIFTEEN

Mrs Reed's comments trail me back to Mr Dowling's personal quarters and plague me. I hadn't really thought about the mutants and why they threw in their lot with the clown. I assumed they were all bad to the bone, that in their twisted wretchedness they'd sought him out. Or maybe they were good people whose minds had been corrupted, unwilling servants who'd been kidnapped and modified. But Mrs Reed's reasons for lending her support to Mr Dowling have made me re-evaluate things.

A few days later Kinslow and a couple of his mutant colleagues drop in on me as I'm exercising, trying to pass the time while knocking my body back into shape. I didn't think I'd ever bounce back to anything like normal when I first arrived here after my mauling at the hands of Dan-Dan, but daily soakings in the vat of blood and brains have worked wonders. I'm not up to gladiatorial standards, and maybe never again will be, but I'm getting stronger every day, almost at the same sort of levels as before I began training with the Angels.

'Looking good,' Kinslow says and it's hard to tell if he's being sarcastic or not.

'Good enough to take you in a fair fight,' I grunt, finishing my press-ups before getting to my feet.

'You probably could,' he says sourly. 'That's why I prefer to fight dirty. Now, if you're done working out . . .'

'Where are we going?' I ask as we head up the stairs. 'To see the babies?'

'No,' he says, surprising me. 'Mr Dowling's noted your restlessness. He wants to show you some things, to get you more involved in our affairs. He meant to take you himself, but he's been called away.'

We weave our way through the maze of rooms, and I'm pleased to note that I'm moving much more fluidly than when I first toured the chambers. I spot some mutants in the middle of a kick-boxing contest. I'd like to stay and watch, maybe even take part to test myself, but Kinslow hustles me forward.

I try to map our route as we proceed. I've been doing this every time I'm led out of Mr Dowling's personal quarters, building up an overview of the complex, looking for possible exit points or places where I could hide. Of course the babies would be able to track me down mentally if I hid, which is a major fly in the ointment, but that doesn't stop me toying with ideas of escape.

Kinslow takes me to an area of the den that I didn't know existed. There are five linked but otherwise isolated rooms. A sign over the door – painted in blood naturally – informs me that I'm about to enter *Mr Dowling's Zoo.*

'It's not a real zoo, is it?' I ask.

'Sure it is,' Kinslow says. 'There are no lions, elephants or anything like that, but plenty of interesting exhibits all the same.'

The *interesting exhibits* are insects, spiders, butterflies, reptiles and the like, dozens of different species stored in a variety of tanks and cages, each room cluttered with them. This is where Mr Dowling stores the creatures that he places in his mouth when he wants to make an impression.

'He doesn't keep an animal in his mouth all the time, does he?' I ask Kinslow as we wander from one glass cage to another.

'Not when he's at home,' Kinslow says, 'but he usually pops something in whenever he's heading up to the streets.'

'Why?' I ask. 'What are they for?'

Kinslow shrugs. 'I'm not sure even he knows. Maybe it makes him feel more alive, to have something living inside himself. Maybe it's just to freak people out when he meets them. Maybe they help him focus. Whatever, it's up to us to care for them. I oversee a small team and we make sure the

temperatures are maintained at the correct levels. We feed the creatures, clean up around the place, keep them in tip-top shape.'

'I wouldn't have pegged you for a zookeeper,' I chuckle.

'I hate it,' he scowls. 'It's a waste of time and resources. But you don't say no to Mr Dowling.'

'Tell me about it,' I grunt.

'You can help us look after them,' Kinslow says.

'So that you can slack off?' I grin.

'I wish,' he sighs. 'I'll still have to come and keep an eye on things. But it will give you something to do and provide you with a chance to get out a bit more.'

I've no real interest in tending to a load of bugs, but this could work in my favour when it comes to plotting an escape. The zoo's situated in a quiet part of the complex. Maybe I could make use of the insects, sneak some out, hit the mutants with them as we're returning to my quarters, startle them, club them senseless in the confusion, slip away without any of the others noticing. Not today, but when I've got the hang of the place, when they're accustomed to me coming and going, when I'm in better shape than I am now.

'I've always been fascinated by spiders,' I lie. 'I'd love to work here and learn more about them. Cheers, Kinslow. This was one of your better ideas.'

'Not mine,' he sniffs. 'Mr Dowling's, like I told you.'

Kinslow continues to show me round, tells me the names of some of the more exotic creatures, explains their needs, how we feed them, what we have to watch out for. He might claim to be a reluctant zookeeper, but he seems more content here than anywhere else I've seen him. For the first time I see the human that he once might have been showing through.

'Can you tell me something?' I ask him as he replaces the top on a tank full of beetles.

He squints suspiciously, guessing from my tone that I don't want to know more about the bugs. 'Depends what it is,' he says.

'Why do you do this?' I ask, prompted by memories of my conversation with Mrs Reed. 'What drew you to Mr Dowling? Why did you let him change you? Why do you follow him?'

Kinslow studies me in silence, debating whether or not to answer. When he sees that I'm truly curious, not searching for something to criticise him for, he says in a low voice, 'I was married once.'

'Oh yeah?' I try to sound happy for him.

'I murdered my wife.'

If I could blink, I would.

'The judge decided it wasn't my fault,' he continues. 'I was declared mentally unhinged. I agreed with the verdict. I hadn't been myself for a long time. I'd been imagining things. I was hearing voices. I wasn't in control.

'They sent me to an institution and doped me up. I was happy, free to hide from the world and what I'd done. I couldn't hurt anyone again. I thought that was it for me. Spend a few decades kicking around the rooms of my prison, then die a lonely, forgettable death.

'Mr Dowling had other ideas. He broke into the asylum. Went through the records and drew his own conclusions. Gathered a selection of inmates and took us with him. I was furious. I wanted to go back but he wouldn't let me. He weaned me off the drugs and taught me to embrace my dark side. He showed me that I'd spiralled out of control because I hadn't understood my true character.

'I was born bad. People often argue about whether we're born evil or have it bred into us. In my experience, it's a bit of both in most cases. But for me it was all natural. I came into this world with my fingers twitching, a destructive spirit from the get-go.

'If I'd embraced my true nature, I could have controlled myself the way I do now, lashed out against those who meant nothing to me, been careful and loving around those who mattered. But, because I tried to be a normal person, I fought my natural instincts and lost. By trying to suppress my violent streak, I ended up killing the woman I loved instead of some random piece of scum.'

'Who are you to decide who's scum and who isn't?' I challenge him.

'Oh, I'm perfectly positioned to make that call,' he

grins bleakly. 'After all, I'm scum myself.' He laughs at my confused expression. 'We are what we are. Some of us are good, some bad, most somewhere in the middle. Mr Dowling thinks we should all live the way we were meant to.'

'So he's happy for killers to parade about freely?' I huff.

'If it's their time,' Kinslow nods. 'It wasn't when I was growing up. If I'd been open about my urges, I would have been identified and dealt with before I could have done any real damage. I fit in now because this *is* a time for killers. The meek and the good have fallen. I don't know what lies ahead, but right now the world's a cauldron of violent madness, ripe for the likes of me and Mr Dowling.

'He taught me that there's a time and a place for all of us. That's why nature bred so many varieties of human beings, the bad and the crazy as well as the good and the sane. If the world doesn't require us, it gets rid of us. If Mother Nature feels like we deserve a play in the pen, she'll pass over the reins of power for a while.'

I scratch my head, staring at the mutant, trying to process what he's telling me.

'Don't sweat it,' he smirks. 'Our time will be short-lived. Order will restore itself. So we should squeeze the most out of the experience while we can, before the good times are ripped away and the boring, decent people rise to the top again. Mr Dowling is only maximising his use of the brief, chaotic period that the world has granted us. That's why he has my vote.'

'Wait.' I stop Kinslow as he turns to link up with the mutants outside and lead me back. 'You keep saying *our, us, we*. I'm not one of you. I'm different. I belong with the good guys.'

'Maybe.' Kinslow winks. 'Or maybe that's just what you want to believe. Ask yourself this — does Mr Dowling love you because you're pure? Or does he see a mirror image in you of his own vile, twisted self?

'Sweet thoughts, cupcake,' he chuckles, saying nothing more as I'm led back to my room in thoughtful, worried silence.

SIXTEEN

Mr Dowling comes to me again a few days after my chat with Kinslow. He doesn't provide me with an explanation for his absence and I don't ask. I've been enjoying life without him – well, as much as a slave *can* enjoy life – going each day with Kinslow and the other mutants to work in the zoo. The creepy-crawlies have turned out to be more interesting than I imagined. I wouldn't fancy looking after them indefinitely, but in the short term they've been a welcome distraction.

The clown does his electrocution trick without

even saying hello, and leads me through more of the deranged labyrinth of his mind. I don't know how many levels there are, and he doesn't tell me when I ask, but he does say that I've already crawled further through the mental maze than anyone else. He's shared more with me than he has with even his closest confidants like Kinslow and the scientists he works with.

I should be honoured, but I can't see him as a liberating hero. I've started to consider him in a different light since my discussions with Mrs Reed and Kinslow, but ultimately he's still a terrorising maniac in my book.

As the clown treats me to deeper insights and nuggets from his past, I summon an image of him and ask the question that is foremost in my thoughts. 'What are your plans for the world?'

His projection is dressed in a pink suit today. He raises an eyebrow and smiles. '*I want to marry you and raise our babies.*'

'But for the world in general,' I press. 'Mrs Reed hopes that the babies will correct humanity's mistakes. Kinslow wants this to be a place where evil people can run wild. What do *you* want?'

The shape in front of me shimmers and Mr Dowling reappears in his clown's outfit. His eyes don't revolve the way they do in the real world, his flesh doesn't ripple and there are no body parts sewn on to the material of his costume, but this is the closest he's come to replicating his usual look inside our mental realm.

'*I want to break free,*' he sings, doing a lousy Freddie Mercury impression.

'I'm serious,' I huff.

'*I don't want to be,*' he counters. '*A serious world is a dull world.*'

'Come on,' I groan. 'I don't ask for much. This is important if you want me to get to know and love the real you.'

He stares at me solemnly, thrown by my suggestion that I might be capable of developing feelings for him. Then he says, '*Albrecht.*'

'What?' I frown.

'*My first name is Albrecht. My parents named me*

after the painter, Albrecht Dürer. He was their favourite artist.'

'Well, that's insightful,' I mutter sarcastically. 'But it hardly –'

'One of his most famous engravings was Knight, Death and the Devil,' Mr Dowling continues. *'My father told me that it was inspired by Psalm 23 — "Though I walk through the valley of the shadow of death, I will fear no evil."'*

Images of recent atrocities flicker through my mind, zombies cutting loose, ripping into people, chewing on brains.

'This world has become an immense valley of death,' Mr Dowling says softly. *'The knight in Dürer's painting had faith to keep him strong, to protect him from the forces of darkness stacked against him, but I lost my faith many years ago. The only way I can bring myself to fear no evil is to become evil. After all, what has a man to fear when he is the personification of fear itself?'*

'That's ... interesting,' I mutter uncertainly.

'You asked me what I want,' he says. *'Here is my honest answer. I want to cruise through the valley and*

feel no fear. To do that, I must continue as I am. I'm confident that our babies will take over this world – it will be our gift to them – but not during my lifetime. I need humanity. I need zombies. I need soldiers and racists. In their chaotic clashes, I find solace. In war, I find joy. As long as this is a world of evil, I have a home in it and I have nothing to fear.'

'Then you're not looking to wipe out humanity?' I whisper.

'*Of course not. If pushed, I would. I feel no attachment to humans, any more than I feel attached to the undead. But ideally I want to keep them all in the game. The world is a far more amusing place with a variety of players.*'

I think about that for a while. 'So you want us to carry on as we are, humans against zombies, stirring up trouble with your mutants wherever you can?'

'*Yes,*' he beams.

'And you want me to be part of your team, to help keep things bubbling over?'

'*Yes!*' he exclaims, then sighs. '*The knight in the engraving rode alone, but I struggle with loneliness. Life* is no fun if you have to face it by yourself. It's much easier and more enjoyable with someone beside you.'

'Then I'll do a deal with you,' I tell him, having already considered this before I started the conversation. 'If you help Dr Oystein destroy the zombies, I'll be your partner.'

'*But I need them,*' he says.

'No you don't. The zombies are what made this a world of evil. If you take them out of it, you won't have anything to fear.'

He shakes his head. '*The living are far more wicked than the undead. We cannot heal the world by remov-ing the zombies. We would simply hand power back to Justin Bazini and those like him, and I would have even more to fear. No deal.*'

I curse, though I never thought it would be that easy.

'*However . . .*' Mr Dowling murmurs and my ears (so to speak) prick up.

'Go on,' I encourage him when he stalls.

'*I have asked a lot of you without offering much in return,*' he muses aloud. '*I thought I had to turn you to my way of thinking. I saw our relationship as a war*' in which I must bend your will to mine and conquer you completely. But if you're open to the idea of a deal ... to compromise ...'

'I might be,' I nod. 'It depends on what you're offering.'

'*I won't wipe out the zombies,*' Mr Dowling says. '*They're an integral part of this world's scintillating mix. But what if I killed some of my followers for you? I could start with Kinslow, murder another hundred or however many you require. How does that sound?*'

'Like a good start,' I chuckle, wishing that Kinslow was privy to this grisly exchange, so that I could relish the look on his face. 'But that's not what I'm after, not unless you're willing to kill them all and either surrender to Dr Oystein or retreat to a cave where you can do no harm.'

'*That's asking too much,*' he tuts.

'What if you returned your sample of Schlesinger-10 to the doc?' I try instead.

Mr Dowling's eyes bulge. '*Never!*' he croaks more vehemently than I expected. '*Are you even madder than me? He will never get his hands on that!*'

'OK, calm down, don't have a cow. I'm just tossing ideas out.'

'*I could kill the rest of the racists for you,*' he says after a minute of thought. '*If you became my wife, we could hunt them down together.*'

'That's a definite possibility,' I grunt. 'We could certainly make that part of the deal. But I'd need more. How about you declare a truce with Dr Oystein and his Angels, swear never to attack them again?'

He frowns. '*But I have not attacked them previously.*'

'Apart from when you tried to kill the doc,' I remind him.

'*That was a long time ago,*' he smiles. '*Water under the bridge. If they come after me, I will defend myself, but I have no interest in assaulting them. I want them to continue as they are. The world needs their kind.*'

He seems to have forgotten about when he sent Billy Burke after the doc in County Hall. I almost remind him, but I feel like we might be close to something big and I don't want to lose the momentum.

'What if you stopped killing people?' I try.

'*But murder is so much fun,*' he protests.

'I'm sure it is,' I growl, 'but it isn't right. I could never give my heart to a man who butchered freely. That's a deal-breaker as far as I'm concerned.'

Mr Dowling strokes his chin thoughtfully. '*I see from your memories that you had a talk with Kinslow recently. So you know my opinion of killers. This is a time for assassins, and I don't believe that people should hide their true colours. It would be hypocritical of me to tell Kinslow and those like him that they should stop slaughtering.*'

'Then there's no point in us taking this any further,' I sigh.

'*I'm not so sure of that,*' he says hesitantly. '*There might be room for a few degrees of negotiation. I enjoy killing, but for me it's a sport, not an obsession. I believe that I could stop if I wished.*'

The clown thinks about it some more, then nods. '*If you become my wife, I'll attempt to put my murderous ways behind me. I won't try to persuade my followers to stop killing, but I will serve as an example. When they see that I have stayed my hand, some of them might stop too. If I find that I can't stay on the straight and narrow, and feel compelled to kill again, the marriage will be declared null and void and I will free you to go your own way. How does that sound?*

It's not as much as I want, but way more than I expected. I mull it over, considering the angles and my options.

'What would I have to do as your wife?' I ask.

'*Be my right arm,*' he answers promptly. '*Support me. Help raise our babies. Offer me a shoulder to cry on.*'

'No funny business?' I press.

'*I'm a clown,*' he grins. '*All of my business is funny.*'

I roll my eyes, unimpressed. 'You know what I mean.'

He crosses his heart. '*I will do nothing to you without your permission.*'

I think it over some more. Maybe his madness has started to rub off on me, but this seems like a good idea. As his wife, I'd be able to exert a positive influence over him. If he stops killing, it will be a massive step forward. Maybe, over time, I could convince him to stop the mutants killing too.

I bat the options back and forth, wondering what Dr Oystein would think. I recall Owl Man's prediction that Mr Dowling would win me over in the end. That makes me consider rejecting him, purely on principle. But it would be childish to turn down the deal just to spite Owl Man.

Finally, throwing up my hands, I snap, 'OK. I'll settle for those terms.'

'*Becky!*' he cries, sweeping me up in his arms and whirling me round. '*You've made me the happiest man in the world!*'

Our minds start to disconnect and we return to our bodies. The clown has picked me up off the floor and is dancing with me in this realm too, his delighted laughter echoing through the corridors of my brain.

Kinslow is lounging by the vat of blood, running his fingers through the liquid, observing the ripples, a dreamy look on his face.

'*Kinslow!*' Mr Dowling snaps at his assistant,

copying me in on his mental commands. '*Stop dawdling. We need a dress. Shoes. A fresh suit for me. The babies must be told and prepared. Letters will have to be written and passed around. So much to think about and do. It would be enough to drive me mad, if I wasn't already.*'

'Master?' Kinslow frowns, not sure what's going on.

Mr Dowling beams, his eyes jitterbugging about even more than usual, leaping from foot to foot as if on hot coals. '*She! She! She!*' he gibbers. Then he gets himself under control for a moment, jabs a bony finger in my direction and cries victoriously, '*Here comes the bride!*'

SEVENTEEN

Mr Dowling prepares for our big day as if it was a royal wedding. He zips round the caverns in a blur, tossing instructions left, right and centre, spurring his mutants into action. Everything has to be redecorated ... we need more lights ... the walls require a fresh lick of excrement and blood ... it has to look festive.

He sends teams scouting for paintings and statues. Just as I've been learning about his mind, he's been learning about mine, and he sees how I've recently become interested in art. He has them pick pieces that he thinks I'll like, eager to impress me. They come back laden with some of the finest works that London has to offer, many from the National Gallery, and set about putting them in place.

Everyone's instructed to look their best. When the mutants have finished ransacking the galleries, they raid department stores and return with stacks of new dresses and suits, more shoes than any woman ever dreamt of, scarves and ties and heaven knows what else.

The babies can't understand why people are so excited. They don't know what a wedding is. As far as they're concerned, we're their mummy and daddy, and that's all there is to it. Ceremonies mean nothing to them. Still, they sense Mr Dowling's glee and respond to it, squealing dutifully whenever they see one of us.

Lots of the mutants eye me suspiciously when I pass. I can tell what they're thinking — she doesn't really want to marry him, it's a scam, we can't trust her. The odd thing is, they're wrong. I'm not ecstatic about this, but I'm more pleased than I thought I'd be. And, while I won't rule out plotting against my horrendous hubby in the future, for now I'm happy with his promise to change his murderous ways. I see this as getting a foot in the door, and for the time being I'm satisfied with that.

I ask Mrs Reed to help me choose a dress, but she says Mr Dowling has already picked one for me. I'm annoyed.

'Grooms aren't supposed to see the dress before the wedding day,' I complain. 'It's not right. He probably went for something disgusting, red and heavy, adorned with guts.'

'Possibly,' Mrs Reed concedes. 'But he is very firm about having this day go exactly the way he wishes. It means a lot to him. He's been planning this for years, ever since you were an infant.'

'Don't you find that a bit . . . *yeurgh*?' I shiver.

She smiles. 'Mr Dowling has nothing untoward in mind. He was attracted to your personality, not your body.' She casts a critical eye over me. 'Which is just as well as you're a poor catch, physically speaking.'

'Yeah, well, you're no oil painting yourself,' I huff, and we share a genuine laugh for one of the very few times in our relationship.

Kinslow is in charge of organising the ceremony. He's under stress, and fusses over the vows as if his life depends on getting the words right. Which it might.

'What about this?' he asks, handing me his umpteenth draft.

I have a quick read and grunt dismissively. 'Too flowery. Keep it simple.'

Kinslow winces. 'Do you think that's what he wants?'

'I'm not sure. But it's what *I* want.'

'I wish he'd never volunteered me for this,' the mutant moans. 'Or that he'd given me clearer instructions. All he said was to jot down the vows and make them good. He's paying close attention to everything else, so why did he brush this off as if it was no big thing, leaving it all to me?'

'I don't think he knows what he wants to say,' I tell Kinslow. 'From what I've seen of his mind, he's dead set on marrying me because he thinks he loves me, but he has no idea what love actually is, or how he should express his feelings. He's like a child in certain ways.'

'Yeah,' Kinslow grumbles, 'but a child who can have my head impaled on a spear if I get it wrong.'

And off he staggers to work on another draft.

Mr Dowling hasn't set a date. He just said we'll get married when everything is ready. He's given an invitation to every mutant and baby, telling them of the *good news* and ordering them to be ready to attend at a moment's notice. He signed each invite, though the style of his signature varies from card to card — if you didn't know better, you'd think they'd been signed by hundreds of different people writing the same name.

I'm nervous now that the train has been set in motion. It seemed like a good idea when we were discussing our deal, a way to turn this wretched situation to my advantage. But the more time passes, the more I start to feel that it's a massive mistake. I'm playing into the clown's hands, doing what he wants. Maybe this is the first step down a slippery slope and, instead of me changing Mr Dowling for the better, he'll change me for the worse.

I study my reflection in a mirror, looking for hints

of evil in my eyes, finding only the same blank expression I've worn since I returned to consciousness. Might this be the start of the end? A few months from now, will I have fallen under the clown's spell? Will I be out on the streets with him, hacking people to pieces, leading the fight against Dr Oystein? Am I poised to become the very thing I most despise?

'You're crazy,' I tell myself. 'Nothing good can come of this. You're trying to control a madman who freely admits that even *he* has no control over himself. Get out now, girl. Kill yourself while you can, while you're still part-way human.'

But I can't. Because if Mr Dowling *does* uphold his end of the bargain, and if I *can* soften him up, it could signal a whole new chapter in this war of the undead. Dr Oystein says that the clown is an agent of the Devil, but maybe I can turn him into an Angel.

I chuckle as I imagine the doc's face if I come waltzing into County Hall, Mr Dowling following me like a lamb, to hand over his vial of Schlesinger-10, leaving the flabbergasted doctor free to uncork his tube of Clements-13, wiping out all of the zombies in the space of a week or two. Of course, the three of us would die too, but myself and the doc are happy to sacrifice ourselves for the greater good. The question is, can I convince Mr Dowling to do the same?

As I'm debating the dilemma, still trying to work out if this is the best or worst idea I've ever had, Mr Dowling creeps up behind me. He's by himself and carrying a few large boxes.

'*My darling,*' he coos inside my head. '*Such a divine little creature.*'

'Save it for your next girlfriend,' I snort. 'I'm not buying. I know what I look like. I'm rough as a pig's arse.'

'*You're a diamond,*' he insists. '*And I will polish you up, to reveal your finest shine.*'

He sets down the boxes and opens the largest, pulling out a white dress.

'Is this my wedding gown?' I ask, expecting an atrocity.

'*Yes,*' he says simply, passing it across. He takes a

step back and strokes the flesh of his cheeks, studying me anxiously, awaiting my verdict.

The dress is a lot nicer than I'd anticipated. Simple
but classy. Nothing too ornate. Exactly the sort of
dress I'd have picked for myself if I'd had the option.
There's a veil too, that attaches to the nails hammered into my scalp, becoming an extension of my
ever-present crown.

'This is damn nice,' I tell him, turning it round to
examine the back.

'*It screamed* you *to me as soon as I saw it,*' he gushes.

'You're a funny sod, aren't you?' I laugh. 'The soft-
est mass murderer I've ever heard about.'

'*Not a murderer for much longer,*' he smiles, opening
the other boxes to reveal a hat, shoes, blue underwear,
a garter. '*I borrowed the garter from Mrs Reed. And the
shoes came from a second-hand shop, so they're old. I
think that covers all of the traditional bases.*'

'What was Mrs Reed doing with a garter?' I frown.

'*I didn't dare ask,*' he smirks.

I look round at all of the items and nod. 'You did
a good job, Albrecht.'

'*I thought so*,' he says. '*But I couldn't be sure. You're happy with everything?*'

'Yeah. It'll be weird wearing something of Mrs Reed's, but I can live with the garter. Just don't try pulling it off with your teeth. Remember what we said — no funny business.'

'*You have my word*,' he giggles, crossing his stomach instead of his heart by mistake. '*In that case, don your robes immediately, Becky Smith.*'

'So that you can see what they look like on me ahead of the big day, in case you need to alter them?' I ask.

'*No*,' he says. '*You must put them on now because I've decided we're going to hold the wedding this afternoon.*'

'Wait!' I cry as he trots off to spread the word. 'I need more time. You can't spring it on me like this.'

But he's not paying attention. He's made his decision and that's it, no room for discussion. I mutter something cutting, then eye the wedding dress nervously, shake my head and start pulling off my clothes.

EIGHTEEN

The wedding takes place in the complex's largest chamber. It's where the mutants usually gather for meals. Unlike zombies, they need to eat food as well as brains.

The tables and benches have been cleared, while fridges, freezers, ovens, microwaves and the rest have been moved to other rooms. The walls are adorned with paintings by Dali, Picasso, Van Gogh. There are several pieces by Dürer, to keep the groom happy, while Seurat's massive *Bathers at Asnières*, my favourite painting since I started to take an interest in such things, is suspended on the wall above the makeshift altar.

191

Mixed in with the paintings are human limbs, lengths of gut twisted into bizarre shapes, and dozens of newly scribbled pictures of myself and Mr Dowling, all done in fresh blood. That's a habit I'll try to knock out of him once we're Mr and Mrs.

The mutants are standing in lines on both sides leading up to the altar, leaving a gap in the middle for an aisle. The babies are ahead of them, gathered round the platform which has been installed for the happy occasion. Everyone looks immaculate in their new garb — well, the babies are wearing their regular white christening gowns, but every item has been freshly laundered.

Owl Man is standing inside the entrance to the room. I'm surprised to see him, but even more surprised to see Sakarias and Rage.

'What are you mugs doing here?' I snap.

'We were invited,' Owl Man says. 'The only guests from the outside world. How could we refuse such an honour?'

'I can't believe this,' Rage snickers, eyeing me in my dress, shaking his head incredulously. He's wearing clean jeans and a smart leather jacket, with polished-up Doc Martens, toebones sticking out of the holes that have been cut for them.

'What?' I huff. 'Didn't think I ever wore dresses?'

'Well, no, now that you mention it,' he laughs. 'But I meant I can't believe you're marrying the so-called spawn of Satan, the enemy of the doctor you love so much, the man you'd dedicated yourself to annihilating.'

'It's complicated,' I mutter. 'I've convinced him to stop killing, but I had to marry him to seal the pact.'

'Ah,' Owl Man nods. 'I wondered how he'd win you over.'

'If you dare say *I told you so*, I'll go for your throat,' I growl.

'I wouldn't dream of it.' He raises an eyebrow at Kinslow. 'Have you been charged with the task of giving the bride away?'

'Not as such,' the mutant scowls. 'I've just been told to get her here on time and make sure she goes through with it.'

'A pity your father didn't survive a bit longer,' Owl

Man says, offering me a sad smile. 'I imagine you always dreamt of him walking you down the aisle.'

'Get real,' I snort. 'I never planned to marry, but if I did I wouldn't even have invited him to the wedding.'

'I doubt that,' Owl Man says. 'You loved him despite his flaws. You must be upset that he cannot be here. Your mother too.'

'Well, I wasn't until you brought it up,' I snarl, but of course that's a lie. How could I not have considered them? Their absence has pierced my heart (or the shadow of it) every day since the riots at Battersea Power Station. I've been missing Vinyl too. But I'm determined to push those sad memories aside and not let anything cast a cloud over today's big event.

And, regardless of everything, how I came to be here and the crazy creep I'm marrying, it *is* an event. I have butterflies in my stomach, or at least the memory of what that felt like. I'm nervous looking at the assembled guests. I want this to go well. It's not the wedding I ever thought I'd be having, but now that I'm here, I'd like it to pass off smoothly.

194

Owl Man studies me as I chew at my lower lip (carefully, so as not to rip it with my new teeth), then coughs politely. 'Master Kinslow, if you don't mind, I would like to offer my services, if Miss Smith judges me an adequate substitute.'

'What are you babbling about?' I frown.

He extends an arm. 'If you have no objections, I'll walk you to the altar. I think every bride should be given away by someone who is truly fond of them, and no matter what you might think of me, I do fit that description.'

I stare at the tall, pot-bellied man suspiciously, wondering if he's mocking me. But there's no sign in his expression that he's trying to play a nasty trick. After a brief hesitation, I smile awkwardly and take the proffered arm.

'But don't think this makes us friends,' I warn him. 'I haven't forgotten your partnership with Dan-Dan or the fact that you keep slaves and experiment on them.'

'I never assumed that you would,' he chuckles. 'Let's call this a temporary ceasefire. Our battle can resume later. For now, let us focus only on the joy that is inherent in a day as significant as this.'

'You're as crazy as each other,' Rage mutters. 'I think the pair of you should marry the clown. Two's company, three's a nuthouse.'

'Now, now, Michael,' Owl Man tuts. 'Be nice or I'll sic Sakarias on you.'

'Not a hope,' Rage says. 'Me and the dog are tight. I think he likes me more than you.' He reaches out to pat the sheepdog's head. Sakarias growls at him and pulls away. 'See?' Rage grins. 'Best of buddies.'

'You and Sakarias can wait here for us,' Owl Man says, then sets off down the aisle, measuring his steps as if he's an expert.

'Have you done this before?' I whisper, matching my stride to his.

'No,' he says. 'But I have enjoyed many marriages on television. I loved a good old-fashioned wedding back in the day.'

We glide along, everyone smiling at us, no dark glances now. Some of the mutants coo and murmur, 'Isn't she lovely?' I can't blush, but I do smile impishly

and lower my head. I'd think this was sickening if I was watching it from afar – I always thought people acted like saps on their wedding day – but, caught up in the middle, I can't help but succumb to tradition. So it turns out I'm a corny romantic who wants to feel special when she weds. So sue me!

Mr Dowling is waiting for me on the platform-cum-altar. It's nothing fancy, just some crates with a few sheets draped across them. But he's had his mutants rustle up a couple of thrones. By the look of them, I think perhaps they hail from the Tower of London or somewhere regal like that. The giant cannon that I spotted when I first came here has been dragged into the hall too — I wonder if he plans to shoot me out of it during the ceremony.

'The paintings are a nice touch,' I tell him as Owl Man and I step up on to the platform, 'but we could have done without the thrones.'

'*Nonsense,*' he says, taking my hand as Owl Man releases me. '*We're worth it!*'

'What about the cannon?' I ask, but he only winks in answer to that.

The clown is wearing a new costume. It doesn't look that different to his everyday outfit, except he's dispensed with the guts and body parts which he normally attaches to the arms and legs. There are no skulls at the end of his huge red shoes either. He's stapled fresh clumps of hair to his head, added more soot to the area around his eyes, and painted the v-shaped channels on his face an even brighter shade of pink than usual. And he's attached an eye to the tip of his nose, something I haven't seen him do in a while.

'Do you really need the eye, today of all days?' I groan.

'*It's my lucky eye*,' he chuckles. '*I like what you've done with your cheeks.*'

'Thanks.' I added glitter to the slits in my cheeks, figuring I might as well highlight my disfiguring wounds rather than try to disguise them. I also polished my elf's ears and coated my fingerbones and toebones with a thick layer of black, before adding some silver stars to the mix. Plus, at the last minute, I cut a hole in the dress around my left chest, to show off the gap where my heart was gouged out. For me, that's as much a part of my signature look as my eyes or mouth. I didn't feel comfortable covering it up.

'*Shall we proceed?*' Mr Dowling asks as Owl Man steps back to stand among the babies.

'Why not?' I smile, and we take our place on the thrones.

NINETEEN

A petrified Kinslow stumbles forward and clears his throat. He's trembling. He stares at the gathered mutants and babies, then glances back at Mr Dowling. The clown waves at him to begin. My betrothed is smiling broadly, but I sense a flicker of impatience in the way he waves. Kinslow must sense it too, because he rushes into his speech.

'Ladies, gentlemen, babies, your presence is welcome on this most momentous of days. We're glad you could make it and we hope you have a great time. As you know, we're here to –'

'Kinslow,' I interrupt. He looks round with surprise. 'Slow down and relax. Nobody's going to attack you.'

'Thanks,' he says with a timid smile.

'Unless you balls it up,' I add with sadistic relish.

He scowls at me, but the dig has done him good. He overcomes his nerves and carries on at a more even pace.

'We're here to celebrate the wedding of Mr Dowling –' The clown stands and points to the big badge on his chest with his name on it. '– to Becky Smith. Or B Smith, as she prefers to be known.'

'Nice one, Kinslow,' I murmur, and he nods smugly.

'Neither party is religious, and we can't have a civil service because we killed all the civil servants.' There's a huge cheer, deep guffaws and applause. 'So I'm going to conduct the ceremony,' Kinslow adds when the crowd calms down. He's grinning like a loon, thrilled at how well his joke went over.

Kinslow settles firmly into his groove. He tells some stories about myself and Mr Dowling, how

202

I'm the mother of the babies – they start squealing, *'mummy. mummy. we love you mummy.'* – and how the clown fell in love with me on the day we first met, when he beheld the glittering jewel of my most mesmerising mind. (Kinslow's words, not mine.)

He goes on to briefly cover our years apart, how I grew to maturity while Mr Dowling was busy building his army of mutants. He throws in a few more jokes, riffing on my rebellious streak and Mr Dowling's insanity. He describes the zombie uprising and downfall of humanity as if it was a plot device in a romantic novel, designed to bring the pair of star-crossed lovers back together. The mutants *ooh* and *aah* in all the right places. Who'd have thought that a cluster of cut-throat villains could be such a shower of sentimentalists?

Kinslow finally gets to the meat of the matter and turns to address Mr Dowling and myself. 'As B knows, I spent a lot of time trying to get this right,' he says. 'I know how important these vows are to you.'

Mr Dowling nods violently, then sticks a finger up

each nostril, picking both at the same time. Kinslow acts as if that's totally normal. Which, for the clown, it is.

'Albrecht Dowling, do you take B Smith to love and to hold, to share your mind and empire with, to rule by your side and hold dominion over everyone here?'

Mr Dowling rolls up the snot he has gathered and flicks it at Kinslow's head.

'I'll take that as a yes,' the mutant grunts, then turns to me. 'B Smith, do you take Albrecht Dowling as your partner?'

I wait for him to continue, but he stops there.

'Is that it?' I frown.

'Well, you said to keep it simple,' he chortles. 'If you want, I can ask if you plan to obey and honour and share your body with him, but I didn't think you'd be into all that.'

'You thought right,' I huff. Then I glance at the homicidal clown. This is my last chance to back out. He'd probably go wild and kill me if I turned him down in front of everyone. And maybe that would be for the best.

But hell, what sort of a girl would I be if I went and spoiled my own wedding?

'I do,' I declare solemnly.

'Then I now pronounce you clown and zombie, husband and wife,' Kinslow declares. At that point there's a booming sound and the cannon shoots out the biggest ball of confetti I've ever seen. It slams into the wall above us and explodes, tiny white flakes drifting everywhere, covering myself and Mr Dowling like snow. As I laugh with surprise and everyone starts clapping thunderously, Kinslow adds with a giggle, 'You may kiss the bride.'

'There'll be no –' I start to retort, but before I can finish Mr Dowling leaps across, rips off my veil, grabs me tight and plants his lips on mine. As I struggle fiercely, I feel him push something into my mouth with his long, black tongue.

Breaking free, I spit it out and spot a thick slug glistening on the floor at my feet.

'You son of a bitch,' I shriek, slapping Mr Dowling as hard as I can.

'*Sorry,*' he chuckles inside my head, flashing me the

closest thing he can get to an apologetic smile. '*I couldn't resist!*'

'Do that again and this will be the shortest marriage in history,' I snarl. But since there's no point blaming the lunatic for his actions, I don't take too much offence, and moments later I link my arm with his and the pair of us step down off the platform to parade among our subjects, accept their congratulations and embark on our life together as a happily – well, *madly* – married couple.

TWENTY

We don't spend too long doing the rounds. I can tell that Mr Dowling is bored now that the ceremony is over. He wants to move on. He forces himself to mingle for a while, since some part of him knows it would be rude to cut out immediately, but he's an impatient bunny.

'I think we should retire for the night and spend some quality time alone,' I tell him, offering him an excuse to leave early.

The clown wrings his hands and nods eagerly, then stands on his toes and waves flamboyantly to everyone.

'We will take our leave also,' Owl Man murmurs, coming forward to kiss my cheek. 'I wish you all the happiness in the world, Becky.'

'Like I've told you before, it's B,' I growl.

'I know,' he smiles. 'But how disappointed would you be if I stopped annoying you now?'

I laugh warmly at Owl Man as he retreats, then give Rage an evil glare, letting him know his card is marked. He flips me the finger and slopes off without saying a word. I don't envy Owl Man his choice of assistant. I trust Rage about as much as I'd trust a sackful of rabid rattlesnakes.

Mr Dowling treats everyone to a final wave then propels me out of the chamber. He's humming something – it's a mix of several different tunes – as he hops along, dragging me with him.

'Where are we going?' I ask, shaking confetti from my scalp and dress.

'*The bridal suite,*' he giggles.

'Slow down,' I snap. 'Remember our rules? There won't be any fun and games tonight.'

'*Of course there will. A wedding isn't a wedding until*

it's been given the full nuptial stamp of approval. But don't worry,' he adds as I get ready to rear up on him. *'This will be a mingling of our minds, not our bodies.'*

'Yeah, well, that's OK then,' I mumble dubiously.

Mr Dowling leads me to a chamber far from his personal quarters and the cavern where we held the wedding ceremony. This feels like it's on the outskirts of the complex, even more removed from the central hub than the zoo.

It's a tiny room, smaller than any of the others I've visited. The walls have been painted white and there's a four-poster bed in the centre. I eye the bed beadily, but then I spot Mr Dowling's electrocuting wand and relax. Seems like he's telling the truth and this is going to be just another mental sharing session. I'm cool with that.

Mr Dowling keeps humming as he powers up the wand. I circle the bed, checking out the rest of the room. It's bare, no flowers or anything else to show it's meant for a bride and groom, but at least there are no body parts lying around.

211

'Hey, we didn't have any flowers at the wedding,' I suddenly note.

'*I was going to pick flowers for you,*' he says, '*but I promised no more killing.*'

'That doesn't extend to the plant kingdom,' I laugh.

'*I see no difference between humans, animals and plants,*' he says. '*A vow is a vow. If I made an exception, I would find it hard to limit myself. Honouring my promise will be difficult. My only hope is to cut out killing entirely.*'

'You know,' I mutter, 'maybe this will work after all. I was sceptical about us – I still am – but we might have a sliver of a chance.'

'*I hope so,*' he says earnestly, pausing to look at me. '*You are my lifeline, the only one who can possibly help me recover my senses.*' He gulps, then flexes his mouth several times. I think he's pulling faces, until he shocks me by moaning softly and doing something I never thought to hear.

He speaks out loud.

'You are my hope.'

The words come out in a croak, barely audible. But I can tell it took all that he had to focus his senses and force his lips to work the way they once did. I'm touched by the gesture, more than I thought I could be.

'You poor bastard,' I cry. 'If I can help you, I will. I can't promise success, but I'll try my hardest.'

The clown sticks his right hand under his left armpit and makes a farting noise. I laugh. He's not mocking me. He just can't help himself. But, with my help, maybe one day he can. I thought I was doing the wrong thing before the wedding, but now I'm positive that I was right to accept his proposal. If I can be the saving of Albrecht Dowling, maybe I can ultimately be the saving of the world itself.

Smiling warmly, I lie on the bed and let Mr Dowling squeeze a sponge over my face. He does it softly, lovingly, and it's water for once, not blood — I suppose any sort of liquid helps conduct the current.

The clown lies down beside me. We stare at one another shyly, and in this quiet moment we're a normal couple on their wedding night.

Mr Dowling strokes my cheek. He's calmer than usual. I want him to speak again, but he doesn't break the silence. I don't think he can. With a smile, he lifts the wand and looks at me questioningly, offering me a choice.

'It's OK,' I tell him, covering his bony, mutilated hand with mine. 'I want to merge with you tonight.'

He nods happily, kisses my hand, then gently presses the wand to my forehead. Electricity shoots through me. The world turns whiter than the walls. I fall happily into the void of our shared consciousness. He opens himself up to me completely. It's a beautiful, blissful moment, one of the sweetest I've ever known.

Then we crash in flames and everything goes to hell.

TWENTY
-ONE

It's clear, as soon as our minds join, that he's granted me access to the very core of his psyche. It's like he strips away everything to reveal his soul to me. He doesn't just share his memories, but his feelings as well, his dreams, his fears. Will I finally see the horror that transformed a good man into a psychotic clown?

There's a rush of images and a swell of emotions, too much to process all at once. But one face is clear in the tsunami — Dr Oystein's. It's the first time Mr Dowling has let me browse any of his recollections of the doc. I'm fascinated to find out what happened between them and how they drifted so far apart.

But as soon as I fix on an image of the doctor, something clicks inside me. I sense my brain automatically switching to a specific track. It's sort of like when I used to focus on a crossword puzzle, but I'm not trying to find a word this time — without knowing how, I'm somehow searching for Schlesinger-10.

I've tried to probe Mr Dowling's brain before, on the trail of the venomous virus. He's always batted away my awkward, amateurish jabs with ease. But this is different. Suddenly, without meaning to, I've become a battering ram. I plough through the clouds of memories and mental barriers, bulldozing everything aside, driven by a force I don't understand to find out where he stores his apocalyptic vial.

My actions shock Mr Dowling. He wasn't expecting a concentrated assault. This isn't the B Smith he's come to know from our previous couplings. It's not the B Smith I know either. I'm not in control of my mind. It's doing things I hadn't planned, things I didn't know I could.

While we're both reeling, stunned by this lightning-fast twist, I zoom in on the resting place of the lethal liquid. Mr Dowling screams wordlessly and I feel him wrench away from me, severing the link between us. I know instantly that I'm in trouble. I've betrayed him, and I now pose more of a threat to him than anyone ever has. The only reason Dr Oystein hasn't come after the clown is that he dares not act as long as his nemesis holds the virus which could wipe out humanity in a matter of days if unleashed.

I now know where the vial is being stored. It's here, underground, in a room which only Mr Dowling knew about before I prised the information from him. He didn't tell any of his minions where it was. He didn't trust them with such sensitive details, not even Kinslow. If Dr Oystein had known that, he could have had the clown assassinated years ago. But there was always the risk that Mr Dowling had left orders for the virus to be released if he was killed.

That risk doesn't exist any more. Mr Dowling's cover is blown. If he lets me walk out of here, I could take the vial with me or just tell the doc to set some snipers on the clown. Either way, Mr Dowling can't afford to let me leave. He can't afford to let me *live*. He'll have to kill me. The difficulty for him is that we're both lying on the bed, zoned out, helpless.

I try to will myself out of the mental zone and back into my body, but it's impossible to rush the process. We usually recover from the shock at roughly the same speed, but sometimes I'm on my feet before him, sometimes it's the other way round.

While I'm waiting for the whiteness to recede, I focus on calming myself down. I can't afford to panic. If the clown recovers before I do, he'll finish me off and that will be that, nothing I can do to stop him. But, if we return to consciousness at the same time, then the one who is more composed will have an advantage.

I tune into soothing thoughts and memories. I try not to think that my life is on the line. I don't worry about wasting this chance to return Schlesinger-10 to Dr Oystein. I'm a bottle floating on top of the sea during a storm. If I get washed ashore intact, all well and good. If I shatter from the force of the waves, so be it.

Heh — the secrets of the universe as revealed by Zen mistress B Smith!

Time normally passes quickly when I'm bonding with Mr Dowling. There's so much going on, so many memories to tap into and exchanges taking place, that minutes fly by like seconds. But he's not interacting with me now – I guess he's busy trying to force his mind back into his body – so time starts to drag. It feels like I've been suspended in this void for hours.

'Come on, come on …' I mutter, imagining a hand and a watch, staring at it as the seconds tick by oh. So. *Slowwwwlyyyyyy*.

Finally the whiteness starts to fade. The material stretched across the top of the four-poster bed comes into focus. As I stare at it numbly, lips opening and shutting as if I'm breathing, I realise that fingers are clenched round my throat. Mr Dowling is strangling me, forgetting, in his haste to kill me, that he might as well be choking my big toe. Hell, I don't even have lungs any more.

I chill and let the clown carry on strangling. I want him to think that I'm still out for the count. My fingers are tingling and shaking the way they always do when I'm recovering. I'm waiting for them to steady. Then I'll strike.

As I'm gathering myself, Mr Dowling pulls back and his face pops into view. He's grinning crazily, but I can see alarm and dismay in his expression. He's just realised the uselessness of what he's been doing. Inside my brain he croaks, '*No good!*'

'Damn right,' I snort as he lets go of my throat and looks for something to stab into my skull.

Mr Dowling's gaze snaps back and his eyes widen — he thought I was still in cloud cuckoo land. He bares his teeth and throws himself forward. But he's too late. The B is back!

As the clown comes for me, I swing a hand at him. The bones which he so thoughtfully grafted on to my fingers slice effortlessly through the flesh of his cheek and he pulls away, screeching.

I realise, as I scrabble after him, that I've never seen the clown in a fight. He hasn't needed to get his hands dirty before, always able to rely on his mutants and babies, as well as the sense of terror which he instils in most people simply through his eerie presence. I know he's a genius. I know he's spooky as hell. But what's he like with his fists?

To my surprise, he's pretty nifty. Whirling like an acrobat, he kicks out at my face and connects with one of my fake ears, which stabs into my scalp. It stings, but I've endured way worse than that in my time. Even if he ripped the ear off, it wouldn't be a biggie. I've been worked over by experts. It takes a *lot* to hurt me now.

Snarling, I throw a punch at the clown's nose. He tries to block my incoming fist, but he's too slow. If it had my full force behind it, I think it would do serious damage, but my hand is shaking, so it only strikes a glancing blow. Still, it pops the eyeball which was pinned to his nose and knocks him aside.

Lurching to my knees, I clutch Mr Dowling and wrestle with him on the bed. We're both grunting like pigs as we struggle to gain the upper hand. If anyone was listening outside, they'd think we were having a wild wedding night.

The clown latches on to my right cheek with his teeth. He shakes his head from side to side and rips off a chunk of flesh. I shriek and punch him in the ribs. He huffs and scratches at my eyes. I try to knee him in the groin, but only catch his thigh. He gets a hand into the hole where my heart should be and gropes around inside my chest.

'Sod this,' I mutter and headbutt him.

He wasn't expecting that. It knocks the wind out of him. He falls away from me, eyes spinning. I raise an elbow and slam it into the side of his neck. He chokes and collapses, eyes bulging. I punch him in the ribs a few more times for good measure. Then I get off the bed, wobble a bit, clutch one of the posts for balance and wait for the dizziness to pass.

When my head is clear and my legs are steady, I study the gasping clown. He looks pathetic. He knows he's in dire straits. He tries to crawl away from me. I flex my fingers, getting ready to punch him again.

Then I spot the wand and smile. Mr Dowling took control of the wand in all of our sessions. He never let me zap him. It was always a case of ladies first, even tonight when he was more tender with me than at any time before.

As the injured clown struggles to regain the upper hand, I turn on the wand and carefully – *lovingly* – press it to his temple. He spasms and his eyes roll. Spit flies from his lips. He collapses. I zap him again. And again. One last, lengthy burst of electricity, enough to put even an elephant out of action.

And that's the end of it. He can't fight back. There are no weapons in the room, but I don't need any. I can drive the wand through the back of his head, or use my fingerbones to dig through his skull. Scrape out every last scrap of brain. Go get the vial of Schlesinger-10. Find my way to the surface. Give the virus to Dr Oystein.

The world is saved. The battle is over. The day is mine.

'That was too easy,' I chuckle.

And, as if that acts as a self-serving jinx, the door

to the room flies open. My head snaps round and I spot the babies outside, filling the corridor as far as I can see. Their eyes are glowing red. Their jaws are gaping, fangs glinting in the flashing glare of a set of Christmas-tree lights.

'*daddy,*' they say softly, staring at the clown. Then their heads swivel and their gaze settles on me. '*she hurt daddy.*'

Before I can say anything to defend myself, they sweep forward into the bridal suite, the way they used to sweep forward in the plane in my dreams, and, in a wave of bloodthirsty white, they attack.

TWENTY -TWO

The babies swarm over me and drive me back on to the bed. They rip at me with their fiercely tapered nails and fangs, shredding the material of my beautiful wedding dress, which quickly turns a crimson shade in many places as blood starts to flow. I scream as dozens of them chew on my arms and legs. A few tear the crown from my head and start tugging on the nails which Dan-Dan hammered into my skull.

My screams intensify as the miniature monsters rip apart the patchwork of skin which Mr Dowling stitched across my metal ribs, then start snapping off the ribs and digging around inside me, pulling out the wires and tubes which had been so recently installed.

I feel like I'm in hell. It was never this painful in my nightmares. I stare wide-eyed at my assailants and beg God to end this soon if He exists.

As the babies burrow through me like oversized worms, one of them leaps on to my face, knocks away the infants who were jerking on the nails in my head and says in its high-pitched voice, '*mummy.*'

The others pause and stare at the dissident. The baby readjusts its stance and I get a fix on its face. 'Holy Moly,' I whimper.

'*mummy,*' the baby with the hole in its head says again, firmly this time.

The others point at Mr Dowling and chant together, '*daddy. she hurt daddy. we love daddy.*'

'*yes,*' Holy Moly says. '*but we love mummy too. yummy mummy. we love mummy forever.*'

'*forever,*' the babies whisper. '*don't leave us mummy. we love you.*'

They're confused. They stare from me to the clown

and back again, fingers flexing, mouths opening and closing.

'Let me go,' I moan. 'Daddy and I had an argument. Parents fight sometimes. It doesn't mean you have to stop loving either of us.'

My voice is gurgly. One of the babies must have bitten through my vocal cords.

The infants stare at me solemnly. Their eyes are still red, but not as red as they were a few seconds ago. Or is that just wishful thinking on my part?

'*mummy,*' Holy Moly says again. The baby bends over and gently kisses my cheek. Its lips come away sticky with my sluggish blood.

With a heavy groan, I wrap my arms round Holy Moly and bury my face in the baby's chest. My body shudders and shakes as I sob tearlessly. At least I won't die unloved if the babies ignore Holy Moly's protests and finish me off. This is a cold, hostile world, and I've lost most of the people who ever cared about me, but I won't perish entirely alone and loathed by all. That's small comfort at a time like this, but any sort of a comfort is a welcome blessing in this wretched day and age.

The babies pull back when they see me wailing. *'mummy,'* they whisper. *'don't cry mummy.'* Then they're all stroking me and making cooing noises, trying to calm me down.

I carry on moaning for a long time, clutching Holy Moly, weeping drily into the fabric of its pure white gown. Eventually, since time is against me, I push myself up and smile weakly at the babies.

'I love you,' I tell them and it's the truth.

'we love you too mummy,' they reply, beaming, eyes returning to their normal white colour.

'I want to stay here and look after you,' I continue.

'forever mummy,' they nod happily.

'But I have to go.'

Their smiles fade. *'don't leave us mummy.'*

'I have to,' I insist. 'There's something very important that I have to do. But I'll try to come back. I promise. You can read my mind. You know I'm not lying.'

'mummy loves us,' they beam. *'we'll come with you mummy.'*

I shake my head. 'I wish you could but Daddy

wouldn't like that. He'll be angry with me when he wakes up. I don't want him to be angry at you as well.'

The babies frown. The sight of every forehead wrinkling cutely at the same moment makes me laugh. I let go of Holy Moly and ease towards the edge of the bed. The babies nudge aside to make space for me.

'You'll have to look after Daddy,' I tell them. 'I hurt him more than I meant to. Stay here with him, wait for him to wake, then take him to Kinslow.'

'*we can take him now mummy,*' the babies say.

I smile shakily. 'No. He needs his rest. I don't want you to move him while he's sleeping.'

What I really mean is that I want to buy some time for myself. In an ideal world, I'd finish off the clown, but I can't harm him while the babies are here, and they'd know if I tried to trick them. If I told them to leave us alone in the room, they'd see what I was planning and that would enrage them again. I wouldn't survive a second attack. I'm barely able to hold myself together after the first.

I get to my feet, reel sickly and grab one of the bedposts for support. I feel as if I'm going to black out, the way I do when Mr Dowling zaps me with the wand, but the moment passes. I'm in agony, bits of myself dripping across the floor, but that's nothing new. I've been torn up just as roughly before. This world seems to take great pleasure in tormenting poor B Smith.

'*mummy?*' the babies ask, concerned.

'I'll be fine,' I wheeze, though I'm not so sure of that. The babies did a swift but punishing job on me. My flesh is torn to ribbons all over, ripped away almost completely from around my stomach. Most of my ribs have been snapped off. My neatly repaired insides are a mess. One of the nails has come out of my head — I can see it on the bed, a scrap of my brain matter dribbling from it. Maybe this time the world has pushed me too far.

If not for the vial of Schlesinger-10, I'd probably lie down and let myself fade. I think I have the power to do that, the sorry shape that I'm in. All that's holding me to this realm is a thin strand of willpower. If

I gave up, I'm sure I'd slip free of this mortal coil, and it would be a relief.

But I'm so close to securing victory over the crazy clown and the armies of the undead. One more push, one final surge. If I find the vial and get it to Dr Oystein, I'll have played my role to its fullest, and I can go gladly into the great beyond.

Soon, B, soon, I tell myself. *You can rest for all of eternity in another day or two. But not yet. It isn't your time.*

'I wish it was,' I sigh.

I know. Me too.

The babies stare at me oddly as I laugh chokingly. nile and blow them a kiss. 'Will you wait for me?' ask them.

'*yes mummy*,' they answer instantly. '*we –*'

'*– love you mummy*,' I chuckle, mimicking their eerie tone. 'Good babies. Look after Daddy for me. Tell him …' I pause, then whisper, 'Tell him I'm sorry.'

As the babies nod, I hobble to the door and glance back at my husband. I really am sorry. After what

233

we'd shared and all that he had promised, I wish it hadn't come to this. If we'd had more time, maybe I could have convinced him to hand over the virus of his own free will. It didn't need to end this way, me turning on him, betraying him, abandoning him on our wedding day. But once I zoned in on the vial's location, it was the finish of all that we could have had. No point mourning lost possibilities. In this life, there's only what is.

I wave weakly to the babies, then stagger into the corridor. Closing the door behind me, I limp through the network of underground chambers in search of the vial that will guarantee the living to victory over the forces of the walking dead, know I have to find it quickly and get out of here before my unconscious beloved recovers his senses and tracks me down and kills me.

To be continued . . .